Courting the Darkness Saga:

Dangerous

By

Karen Fuller

World Castle Publishing

Karen Fuller

World Castle Publishing
Pensacola, Florida

Copyright © Karen Fuller 2012
ISBN: 9781938961403
First Edition World Castle Publishing November 1, 2012
http://www.worldcastlepublishing.com

Licensing Notes

Cover: Karen Fuller
Photos: Shutterstock
Editor: Maxine Bringenberg

Karen Fuller

Acknowledgements

I'd like to give a special thanks to authors Kathi S. Barton and Joann H. Buchanan for assisting me with the advanced copies and giving me their valuable opinions.

Chapter One

The rays of the early morning sun slowly made their appearance in the dark alleyway, and the darkness fled to the shadows. Drake Bouvier stood in the doorway of the warehouse, rubbing an amulet between his fingers. A witch, Desiree Dupuis, had blessed many such amulets for Drake. The amulets gave vampires the ability to withstand the sunlight without harm. Drake was torn as to whether to risk walking into the sunshine, or to let someone else be the guinea pig. After all, he was king; what if her spell didn't work? "Desiree swore to me that this would work," he remarked under his breath.

His bodyguard, Sean Devereux, rushed to the open door. "Did you call me, sire?" Glancing at the open door nervously, Sean was careful to keep away from the light.

Drake continued to stare at the brightening alleyway and sighed heavily. "No, Sean. I was talking to myself." He tore his eyes away from the alleyway to look at Sean. "Mica and Desiree haven't left yet, have they?"

"They left about fifteen minutes ago, sire; when you told them that they could leave, Mica wasted no time in getting her out of here."

7

Some of the tension eased out of Drake's mood and he laughed. "He was afraid I would change my mind and command his mate to stay here. He really does hate it here."

"I'm glad," Sean grumbled under his breath.

Drake laughed harder. "He only goads you because you won't stand up to him, you know. It's the same with Desiree. She intimidated you earlier because you let her."

Sean's mouth dropped open. "Did you see what she did to that witch hunter, Hargrove?" Drake nodded. "She turned that poor bastard into a rat."

Drake stopped laughing and frowned at the mention of Jason Hargrove. That witch hunter had been a thorn in his side for the last week. "I would have killed him!"

"I know you would have." Sean shook his head and then leaned against a far wall. "But that witch Desiree creeps me out."

Drake lifted an eyebrow at Sean's comment. "Get a spine, Sean." Drake was irritated at his bodyguard's fear of a mere woman. In his opinion bodyguards were supposed to be fearless. He himself was the king of all the vampires in Louisiana and was reputed to be ruthless and unforgiving. The vampires with good sense feared him; those that didn't died. If Sean hadn't been so loyal and followed orders so well, he would have disposed of him years ago. He glared at Sean and continued, "Underneath it all, she's still just a woman."

"Humph…a woman with a mean temper and a taste for vengeance."

"Desiree and Mica are well matched. Our kind only finds one mate in a lifetime. With Mica preferring the life of a rogue, it's amazing he found a mate at all."

"What are the odds of finding a woman with the same temperament?"

Drake shook his head. "I don't know, maybe one in a million." He smiled. "They make a formidable team. I'm glad they're on our side."

Sean laughed. "And it doesn't hurt to have both of them under your royal thumb of command, either."

Drake chuckled and nodded in agreement. "True—true." He turned his head to stare out into the now bright alleyway. He crossed his arms over his chest and leaned into the doorframe. He wanted to step out into the sunshine. It had been over three hundred years since he last felt the rays upon his face. His kind had been cursed to stay in the shadows or die a fiery death in the light. That was the reason that he had captured Desiree in the first place. She possessed great powers as a witch, and he had commanded her to come up with a spell to free him from the darkness. The amulet he now wore around his neck was the fruit of her efforts. He knew that it should work. Desiree had given Mica and Denise amulets and they worked for them, but still....

"Sire, why are you standing in the open doorway? Are you trying to kill yourself?"

"Hardly," he remarked dryly and pushed himself away from the doorframe. "I'm trying to decide if I trust Desiree's witchcraft enough to step out the door."

Sean's eyes rounded. "Did you let her cast a spell on you?"

He nodded as he continued to stare wistfully out into the bright street. "I would give my right arm to be able to go outside now. Can you imagine the possibilities for us? To no longer be creatures of the night? From the day I became a vampire, some three hundred years ago, I have missed the sun."

Sean crossed his arms over his chest and raised an eyebrow skeptically. "If you would give your right arm, then

9

do it. That would be one sure-fire way to see if her spell worked or not." Drake hesitated and Sean rolled his eyes and goaded, "Now who needs to get a spine?"

Drake growled, grabbing Sean by the throat, and slammed him hard against the wall. "You do not speak to me, your king, in that manner!"

Sean swallowed hard. "Uh, I'm sorry sire. I, uh, spoke out of turn. It won't happen again."

Drake released his throat. "Speak to me in that manner again, and I will throw you out in the sunlight without an amulet," he grumbled sourly, then paced back and forth in front of the door for a few strides in agitation.

Sean rubbed his throat gingerly. "I meant no disrespect."

He glared at Sean, then shook his head. Looking back at the open doorway once more, he took one tentative step. Finally, taking a deep breath, he closed his eyes, spread his arms wide, and stepped out into the sunlight. He stopped hesitantly; surely he didn't step far enough. He took one more step, and when nothing happened he opened his eyes. Drake was standing in the full sunshine. Laughter rumbled from his chest. "Desiree, I could kiss you!" he shouted into the empty alleyway.

"I told you, sire, Desiree left with Mica."

Drake rolled his eyes and frowned at his bodyguard. "I'm beginning to understand Mica's opinion of you." He shook his head and proceeded to walk out of the alleyway toward the street.

"Sire, where are you going?" Sean shouted, somewhat panicked.

"I don't know," he shouted back. "I'll be back when I get back."

Chapter Two

Sherry Lambert opened her eyes to the phone ringing shrilly in her ear. She picked up the alarm clock and looked at the time...7:30 a.m. Closing her eyes, she blew her hair away from her face in exasperation. "Who could be calling me at this ungodly hour in the morning?" Opening a bleary eye, she glared at the LCD but didn't recognize the number. Patience at this time of the morning was a stretch for Sherry. "Hello?"

"Hello, Sherry?"

Sherry yawned into the receiver. "Yes, this is Sherry. Who is this?"

"Sherry, it's me, Desiree."

She sat up quickly in alarm. "Desiree, is there anything wrong?"

She heard Desiree laugh softly into the phone's receiver. "No Sherry, nothing's wrong. You told me I owed you the whole story when I got back. Well, I'm back."

"Boy, you're up early."

"I haven't been to bed yet."

She blinked hard a few times trying to wake up, and stifled another yawn before she spoke. "Okay, so tell me what happened?"

"Not over the phone. I want you to come to me, so that I can show you where I'm living now."

11

"You've moved?"

"Yeah, I lost that dumpy apartment."

"Oh—okay. Do you need me to come over now?"

"Yeah, we need to talk about coven stuff, too."

"That's good. Everyone's been asking about you. Where are you?"

"It's the beige two story stucco mansion just off of Bourbon Street, in the Vieux Carre area."

Sherry's mouth gaped. "That two story *mansion* with the manicured lawns? Did you say mansion?"

Desiree laughed. "Yes, that would be the one."

Sherry threw back the covers in excitement, draping her long slender legs over the side of the bed. She had been dying to hear this story since Desiree had woke her up at two o'clock in the morning a couple of nights ago. "I'll be right over. I've got to hear all about this."

"Good, you can eat breakfast with me. Bye Sherry, I'll see you shortly."

"Bye, Desiree."

She clamped the cell phone shut, then ran her fingers through her silky brown, shoulder length hair and eased out of bed. Once on her feet, she stretched her slender five foot nine inch frame. As her mind raced over the telephone conversation, she put a pout on her beautiful heart shaped face, dolefully shaking her head as she glanced over her shabby furnishings. "Huh—she said mansion. If I was to be so lucky," she mumbled under her breath. Making her way into the kitchen, she put on a two-cup pot of coffee to brew, then glanced wistfully at the loaf of bread next to the toaster. She was hungry, but Desiree had promised her breakfast.

Shadow, her black cat and familiar, jumped up on the counter to greet her. Sherry smiled and scratched the cat behind the ears. "How's Mommy's baby this morning?

Hum?" Shadow immediately began to purr and rubbed up against her affectionately. Sherry laughed. "Okay, okay, I'll feed you. Come on now, get down from the counter. You know better." She picked the cat up off the counter, kissed the top of his head, and placed him on the floor. She opened the cabinet and took out a can of cat food, emptied the contents into the cat's dish, then placed the dish on the floor. "Here you go sweetie, enjoy."

Sherry poured herself a cup of coffee and took it with her into the bedroom. Taking a gingerly sip, she let the hot liquid warm her, then smiled in appreciation. Placing the coffee cup on the dresser, she ran her hands briskly over her chilled arms. February in New Orleans was cold and the hot coffee did its job.

Sherry stepped into the closet to thumb through her clothes. Shadow had followed her to the doorway, then jumped on Sherry's bed, staring expectantly. Sherry glanced at Shadow, shrugging at the cat's expression. "What does one wear to visit a mansion?" she asked the cat. Shadow tilted his head and stared at her with his large, green, intelligent eyes. "It's just Desiree, silly. It's not like I have a hot date or anything." She stopped and sighed. "I wish I had a hot date. I could use some fun and excitement for a change." She reached into the closet and took out her white miniskirt and black formfitting sweater. Turning to her cat with a big smile, she said, "What do you think, Shadow? Is it nice enough to wear to some fancy mansion uptown?"

Shadow lowered his head, narrowing his eyes in disapproval.

Sherry lifted her eyebrow at her pet's response, pointing her finger at the finicky feline. "You, sir, need to stop looking at me like you don't approve. I think I'm going to be meeting her rich new boyfriend. I don't need to show up in blue jeans

13

and a ratty sweatshirt." She bit her bottom lip and smiled at Shadow excitedly. "Maybe he's got a handsome, rich friend. A girl can dream."

The cat sneezed, jumped down from the bed, and left the room with his tail raised haughtily in the air. Sherry narrowed her eyes at Shadow's abrupt exit. "Traitor," she grumbled under her breath.

Tossing the outfit on the bed, she reached for the coffee cup. Wrapping her fingers around the cup she noted that it felt cold. She hesitantly took a sip and scrunched up her face. "Yuck!" She took the cup back into the kitchen and dumped it into the sink, and clucked her tongue as she watched the dark liquid flow down the drain. "I didn't need it anyway," she shrugged to herself, and reached over and flipped the switch off on the coffee maker. "Desiree said we would be having breakfast. I'll just have coffee with her."

As she pushed away from the counter, her stomach growled. She looked up at the clock; it was 8:15. *I better hurry; Desiree doesn't like to be kept waiting*, she thought.

Rushing back to the bedroom, she peeled her sleeping shirt off as she went, then tossed it into the laundry basket as she hurried by. A quick shower and fifteen minutes later she was out the door.

***

Parking her old beat up Ford in front of the mansion, she gaped at the house through her cracked windshield. The house was huge—a two story beige stucco, just as Desiree had said. *This place must have fifteen bedrooms, and probably just as many bathrooms*, she thought. Drawing her lips together in a thin line, she said, "I bet a butler answers the door, too. This better be the place, or these people are going to think I'm nuts."

14

About the time she opened her car door, the front door opened and Desiree stepped outside. Her friend had thick auburn hair that framed her heart shaped face and fell past her shoulders. She had large brown eyes, high cheekbones, and soft plump lips. She was wearing tight hip-hugger jeans, a tight red form fitting sweater, and a black leather jacket.

Desiree smiled hugely as she approached Sherry. "It's about time you got here." Her voice was full of excitement.

Sherry stepped out of the car and smiled back. "What do you mean? I took the fastest shower in history."

"I'm just teasing you—and—well—I guess I'm excited too."

Sherry walked up to Desiree and gave her a hug, then her friend ushered her into the house. She looked around the lush massive room with wide eyes. "So, is this guy the same guy you were with in Tennessee?"

"Yeah, it's the same guy." They walked over to the couch and sat down.

"If I remember correctly, his name is Mica, right?"

Desiree nodded, her eyes sparkling with a happiness that Sherry didn't miss. "There doesn't seem to be anything wrong with your memory," Desiree said. "Oh, by the way, thanks for calling Agatha. I don't think she would have let me in her shop if you hadn't called first. She took one look at Mica and almost didn't open the door."

That's an odd thing for her to say about her boyfriend, she thought, so she raised her eyebrow skeptically, and said, "Okay—now you really have me curious. Why wouldn't she let you in because of your boyfriend?"

Desiree flushed, then looked away. "I guess I need to introduce you to Mica before I tell you my story." She patted Sherry's knee. "Sit tight, I'll be right back."

She was only gone a minute, but nothing Desiree could have said would have prepared Sherry for the sight of them walking back into the room together. Her mouth dropped open when she looked up and saw the six foot seven god before her. He was all muscle. His wavy black hair framed his ruggedly handsome face, and his eyes, a startling blue, were framed by lush black lashes. Sherry caught her breath when he smiled, had to consciously close her mouth before they considered her rude, then did a double take when she suddenly realized he had fangs.

Desiree looked up at Mica and grinned. "Sherry, this is Mica."

Sherry swallowed hard. "Desiree—uh—I think your boyfriend here is a—a—a vampire."

Desiree laughed at her reaction. "Yes, he is."

The color drained from Sherry's face.

"Sherry, I think I need to tell you the story from the beginning. I think you'll understand."

Sherry cleared her throat and couldn't quite meet Desiree's eyes...she suddenly feared for her best friend. Witches didn't associate with vampires, unless—her heart sunk at the only conclusion she could come to. "Desiree, you aren't a vampire now, are you?"

Desiree laughed harder. "No, not hardly."

She let out her breath in a rush. "Good. That's a relief." She looked into her eyes. "I want the whole story."

Desiree looked up at the ceiling as she thought back. "Wow, it's only been a week." She then tilted her head and began. "Some of this story will be a little unbelievable, but listen with an open mind."

Sherry gestured to Mica. "I doubt it will be *that* unbelievable. You have proof sitting here in front of me, so just spit it out."

"You know my situation, Sherry." She nodded. "Word of my true age leaked out. My former landlady snooped through my things and discovered that I was a hundred and twenty-five year old witch and started running her trap." Sherry's mouth dropped open as Desiree continued. "About a week ago I received a summons for a command appearance from Drake Bouvier, the local vampire king." Desiree laughed. "You know me. I tried to get out of it." Sherry smiled. "Drake sent one of his guards to hunt me down."

"So this vampire king, Drake, sent Mica after you?"

She chuckled. "Yes and no." Sherry inclined her head for her to continue. "Mica is not one of Drake's guards. Drake sent his guard Sean after me. Believe me, at the time, Sean was intimidating as hell."

"So, what did this Drake want from you?"

"What he wanted had to do with the phone call I made to you that night. Drake wanted me to cast a spell so that they could withstand the sunlight."

Her mouth dropped open again. "Desiree, that's not possible."

"Sherry, as the leader of our coven, haven't I always taught you that with magic, anything is possible?"

"Yes, but it's never been done."

"Desiree has done just that," Mica said.

"Okay, I'm confused. If Mica's not Drake's guard, then how did you two meet?"

"Drake didn't give me much choice about casting that spell for him, but I somehow convinced him to let me go back to my apartment to get my things. I was all packed and ready to go when Jason Hargrove, the witch hunter, snuck up behind me and knocked me out with chloroform." Sherry's mouth dropped open again as Desiree continued. "Jason trussed me up like a Thanksgiving turkey and carted me off to Salem to burn."

"Oh my God, Desiree…how did Jason find you?"

"Again, I blame my nosy landlady. Drake sent Mica and his friend Caleb to rescue me."

"Is Caleb a vampire too?"

She shook her head. "No, Caleb's a shape-shifter. I've seen him turn into a ferret and a black panther."

Sherry noticed how close they were sitting next to each other, and she smiled. "It looks like it must have been love at first sight."

Mica laughed at her assumption. Desiree flushed and laughed lightly. "Hardly," Desiree said. She glanced up and winked at Mica. "Oh, I admit there was a mutual attraction from the start, but in the beginning I was afraid of him. He was moody as hell and became angry because he thought I was judging him because he was a vampire. Not to mention the fact that he wasn't looking for a relationship." She shrugged helplessly. "Sherry, you know me. I don't like to be ignored."

Sherry laughed in agreement, shaking her head. "Okay, what took you so long to get back?"

"Mica wanted to flush Jason out, so we hid in the Forbidden Caverns for a few days."

"So you two took the advantage of being alone with no interference."

Desiree flushed again, then cleared her throat. "Hardly."

Sherry raised an eyebrow at that. "What's that supposed to mean?"

"I mean it wasn't all smooth sailing. Caleb was attracted to me too." Sherry's mouth dropped open yet again. "Caleb is not one to take a straight *no* for an answer."

"Did they fight over you?"

"Yes and no."

"Okay, I'm confused again."

Mica laughed. Desiree cleared her throat. "Caleb took off to a bar and got drunk. While he was there he managed to find an unusual drinking partner." Sherry nodded for her to continue. "Caleb didn't know he was partying with Jason Hargrove."

Sherry rolled her eyes. "My God, girl, what happened then?"

"I cast that spell for Drake, and gave an amulet to Mica. The spell worked beautifully. Caleb came back from his binge and was acting weird. We all went to a truck stop to take showers and Jason started stalking us. We hurried back to the cavern, only to discover that Jason had struck again and torn the cave apart looking through our things. Mica went outside to run a patrol, and Caleb decided to take advantage of Mica's absence and tried to force himself on me."

Sherry grimaced. "I take it that that didn't go over too well."

"No, it didn't. I rammed my knee in his groin, then he decided that he was going to attack me as a panther. That's when they fought. Mica kicked him out and put him on a bus back to New Orleans."

"Wow, I bet you were glad that was over."

She laughed at her assumption. "It was far from over." Sherry tilted her head in question. "It seems that when Caleb was drinking with Jason, Jason gave Caleb the bright idea to call one of Mica's old girlfriends to run interference. Denise showed up within hours after sending Caleb away."

"Oh no, not the long lost girlfriend routine." Her shoulders shook with laughter. "Did you fall for it?"

She nodded. "Yes, I did."

Mica put his arm protectively around Desiree and spoke. "I almost killed Denise over that. I tried to convince Desiree it was all a lie, but she wouldn't listen to me. You see, Desiree had put herself in a protective circle and I couldn't get anywhere near her." Sherry laughed. "I had to convince Denise to tell Desiree the truth."

Sherry looked into her friend's eyes, grinning slyly. "What did you do to her?"

She laughed. "Nothing at first, but when she laughed and thought the whole situation was funny…." She bit her lip and looked a little guilty. "I threw a fireball at her."

"Good for you. Did you knock her on her butt?"

"No, she dodged it."

"Well, did you at least make her leave?" They both shook their heads no. Sherry's eyes rounded. "Why the hell not?"

"Because she was a vampire and the sun had come up, and it really wasn't her fault. Caleb had called her and talked her into it," Desiree remarked, and Sherry rolled her eyes. "Besides, that wasn't the end of the mess."

"No, let me guess…Caleb came back," she remarked dryly.

"Yeah, he got back just in time to hear me tell Denise that I didn't have any feelings for him."

"Ouch, I bet that didn't go over too well."

"No it didn't." Desiree blew out a breath, then frowned. "I like Caleb as a friend, and I didn't like hurting his feelings." Mica squeezed her hand for support. "Caleb can be annoyingly persistent. If you push him away, he just keeps coming back for more." She held up her hand and counted off on her fingers. "I had punched him, took him down with a knee to his groin, and took him down with a fireball, and he wouldn't take no for an answer. Mica had to threaten to kill him for him to take me seriously and stop. Most guys see me coming and run in the other direction. I am not used to being pursued that ardently. It was kind of creepy."

"Wow, that was some adventure."

"It didn't end there." Sherry rolled her eyes again and waited for her to continue. "We had decided enough was enough, and it was time to come back to New Orleans. We packed the Express Van, and all I had left to do was to retrieve the blessed amulets I had hidden and we were going to be on our way."

"You didn't leave as planned?"

"We didn't get the chance. Jason Hargrove struck again."

Sherry grimaced. "What did he do this time?"

"Mica is a rogue vampire. It means he lives here in Drake's domain under Drake's good graces. He is allowed to live away from the rest of the pack as long as he leaves his services open to the local vampire king. We weren't in Drake's domain, which means by vampire law he could be killed by another clan on sight. Jason turned him in to the local vampire clan and they took them all prisoner. They were to die at dawn when the sun rose."

"They didn't take you?"

"No, I was in my circle and they couldn't touch me."

"We need to get together and cast a spell to take care of Hargrove. He's a pain in the ass."

Desiree winked at Sherry. "I took care of Hargrove. He can't hurt any of us ever again."

"Did you kill him?"

Desiree laughed harder at Sherry's reaction. "No, I turned him into the rat he is, and I put a twist on the spell to make it permanent."

"So, what did you do after the vampire clan carted the others off?"

Desiree opened her mouth to answer when there was a pounding on the front door. She shut her mouth and looked at Mica, puzzled. "Does anyone know you're back?"

He shrugged. "Maybe it's Caleb." He stood up from the couch. "I'll be right back."

They both watched him walk to the front door. "He's hot," Sherry whispered to Desiree.

"You don't have to whisper," Desiree chuckled. "He can hear you perfectly, so don't say anything to me now that you don't want him to hear."

Sherry flushed in embarrassment. "He heard that?"

Mica laughed and said, "Yes, he did."

She rolled her eyes. "Give a girl a little warning next time." Desiree laughed again.

Mica opened the door and stared in disbelief.

"Hello Mica. Aren't you going to let me in?"

Chapter Three

Mica opened the door wider and stepped aside. "Come in." His voice held a hint of caution. "In the past when you wanted to see me, you always sent one of your lackeys. What's the big emergency that you thought you had to come personally?"

Drake raised an eyebrow at his tone. "Hello to you too." His voice held just as much sarcasm. "Actually, I came to see Desiree."

Desiree jumped up from the couch to defuse the situation developing at the front door. "It's Drake," she whispered to Sherry. "I'll be right back." She hurried to the front door.

Up to this point Sherry had been listening to Desiree's story with an open mind, but her mind still held some doubts as to what she could logically accept to be real. The idea of a genuine vampire clan and shape shifters living in New Orleans seemed a little farfetched to her. Her mind still rejected the idea, and she would have to be convinced that all this was real, but for the moment, she wouldn't argue the points with her friend.

She stood and faced the front door. The new visitor, Drake, now commanded all her attention. In her mind, another powerful god had just suddenly appeared from nowhere, and she felt a sudden, instant attraction. She didn't see anything she didn't like—she admired every detail. He had long raven-black hair, piercing, hypnotic blue eyes, high cheekbones, a straight nose, a firm square jaw, and a strong sensual mouth. He didn't tower over Mica, but he was certainly his equal. Her eyes traveled the length of his strong, muscular body. When her gaze finally made it back up to his strikingly handsome face, their eyes locked and he smiled. She caught her breath at being caught staring, but she couldn't summon the will to look away.

"Drake—Drake!" Desiree snapped her fingers a couple of times in front of his face, with no reaction. Looking up at Mica, she shrugged, crossed her arms over her chest, and cleared her throat loudly. "Earth to Drake," she remarked sarcastically. When he still didn't respond, she turned to follow the direction of his gaze and saw Sherry. She looked back up at Mica and blew out a frustrated breath. "This is great—just great." Slamming her hands on her hips, she stepped in front of him, successfully blocking his view of Sherry. She locked eyes with him. "You can't have my friend," she remarked firmly.

He crossed his arms over his chest and cocked an eyebrow at her. "You are in a bold mood today," he growled.

Mica grabbed her by the arm and tucked her protectively behind him. She tried to step around him, but he held her back. She poked her head around his shoulder. "I mean it Drake. You can't have my friend."

"Desiree!" Mica snapped in a harsh whisper.

"Mica, I can handle...." She paused when he turned around and shot her an angry glare. "Uh, I mean...." She glared back at him. "Mica, that's just not fair."

"Mica, you need to control your mate," Drake growled. There was a shocked intake of breath from across the room, and he locked eyes with Sherry again. He softened his tone. "Desiree, introduce me to your friend."

"Mica, do I have to?" she whispered fiercely.

"Yes," he whispered back.

She opened her mouth to object, but Mica stopped her. "We'll talk about this later. Remember we are only allowed to remain here, together, by his good graces. He could always order you go back to the warehouse to live."

She closed her eyes and sighed heavily in resignation. "I'm doing this under protest," she whispered stubbornly. "I don't want to jeopardize what we have." He nodded.

Desiree stepped around Mica. "Come in, Drake. I'll introduce you to my friend, Sherry." He nodded and followed her into the great room. She smiled at Sherry and gave her a 'brace yourself' look. "Sherry, this is Drake Bouvier. Drake, this is my friend, Sherry Lambert."

He took Sherry's hand in his and smiled, but he directed his question at Desiree. "Is she an immortal witch like you?"

Sherry sucked in a shocked breath. "I can speak for myself." Her voice was sharp and sarcastic. "I am a witch, but hardly immortal."

"Another witch, this is excellent." His smile broadened. She tried to take her hand back, and he gripped her fingers tighter. He glanced at Desiree. "You will work on a spell to make her immortal too." Desiree's mouth dropped open at his outrageous demand.

Sherry sucked in her breath again and successfully dislodged her hand. "She will not do any such thing." Anger tinged her voice. "Who do you think you are, ordering my best friend around like that?"

He raised an eyebrow to her sudden outburst, but the smile never left his face.

Desiree clamped her mouth shut. She rubbed her temples at the sudden tension headache she had. "Sherry, it's okay. Calm down."

"I am her king," he remarked as if stating the obvious. Sherry's mouth went slack with disbelief. "Desiree and Mica are my subjects."

She glanced at her friend for confirmation, and Desiree nodded.

Desiree cleared her throat before she spoke. "He is king of this region's vampires." She blew out a breath and continued reluctantly. "Mica is one of his subjects." Drake opened his mouth to interrupt, and she held up her hand. Mica walked up behind her and slipped his arm around her shoulders. She leaned into him. "I am Mica's mate, so that makes me one of his subjects as well."

Sherry looked frantically around the room. "Where is it?" she demanded. "I know it has to be around here somewhere."

"Sherry, what are you looking for?"

"That damned hidden camera."

"Hidden camera?" She rubbed her temples again. "I don't know what you are referring to—"

Sherry crossed her arms over her chest. "This is all so absurd that it has to be a joke, or some weird reality TV show." She searched her friend's eyes again for confirmation.

She shook her head sadly. "I'm not kidding Sherry. A lot has changed in the past week."

Sherry's mouth dropped open and her eyes grew wide as her friend's words sunk in. Then she locked eyes with Drake. He smiled and she noticed his fangs for the first time. Up until that moment, the term 'vampire' hadn't really registered to her as being a reality. The color left her face. "You're a—a...." She swallowed hard. "A vampire?" Black spots suddenly clouded her vision.

"Yes I am…." His voice faltered when she swayed on her feet.

"Drake, catch her!" Desiree shouted.

Sherry barely heard her. The room faded into a black void.

Karen Fuller

Chapter Four

Drake caught Sherry before she could hit the floor. Effortlessly he lifted her unconscious body and held her in his arms. Her head lolled against his shoulder. "I thought witches knew about us," he remarked to Desiree.

She shrugged. "Sure, we knew about the existence of vampires. I just don't think she had ever met one before." She gave Mica an uneasy look. "I hadn't until last week."

Drake looked down at Sherry's unconscious form in his arms. Concern for her creased his brow. "Why isn't she waking up?"

Desiree shrugged again. "She's had a shock. She'll wake up in a minute—or two." Her eyes grew wide as she observed the tender look on Drake's face as he gazed down at Sherry, and how gently he was holding her. "Drake, why don't you put Sherry down on the sofa?"

He tightened his possessive grip on Sherry as he looked back up at Desiree. "No." He turned his head to gaze back down at Sherry.

Sherry's eyes fluttered open at the tight squeeze she received, and she found herself gazing into startling blue eyes that were mere inches from hers. Her heart slammed frantically in her chest as fear gripped her. "Am I still me?" she said in a small voice.

Drake furrowed his brows in concern. "That's a strange question, even for a witch. I caught you before you could hit your head, so I don't understand your question. Who else would you be?"

She swallowed hard. "You didn't bite me, did you?"

He grinned. "No, but I can if you want me to."

Her eyes bugged as she struggled in his arms. "No, I don't want you to!" She pushed on his chest with her hands. It was unmovable, just like pushing against a brick wall. "Put me down!"

He broadened his grin as he gently put her back on her feet. "You sure are a bossy little thing. I like your spirit."

She flushed as she straightened her short skirt, then glanced at Desiree and Mica in embarrassment. "What just happened?" she whispered fiercely to Desiree.

Desiree bit her lip and shrugged apologetically at her friend. "You fainted." Sherry's eyes rounded again at Desiree answering her question out loud. Desiree shook her head at Sherry's expression. "Sherry, I told you earlier that they have excellent hearing. There's no need to whisper. They'll hear you anyway."

Sherry closed her eyes in mortification as Desiree's words sunk in. *I've gotta get out of here.* Her eyes flew open, she squared her shoulders, and she made a conscious decision to salvage what was left of her dignity. "I haven't eaten anything since lunch yesterday. I'm sorry if I alarmed anyone. I must have gotten light headed."

Desiree took the cue. "I'm sorry Sherry. We got to talking and I had forgotten about breakfast. I can have the servant whip something up for us."

She shook her head. "Why don't you and I go out and get breakfast and let these guys talk. *We* need to catch up."

Desiree glanced at Mica, shrugged, then turned back to Sherry and smiled. "Sure Sherry, I'll just go upstairs and grab my purse. I'll be right back." She left her with the guys.

Mica nodded at his servant, Charles, from across the room. He nodded in acknowledgement and went outside.

Sherry focused her eyes on an invisible spot on the sofa, being careful not to make eye contact with either vampire.

Drake inclined his head to her. "Ever since I met Desiree, I find you witches fascinating. I would really like to get to know you better."

Her eyes snapped up to his in alarm. "Huh?"

He chuckled softly. "Why do you two always lose your vocabulary around me?"

Desiree walked back into the room with her bag on her shoulder. "I do not lose my vocabulary when I'm around you, Drake."

He threw his head back and laughed. "That's not true and you know it. That first day when Sean brought you to my chambers, you hardly said two words."

She nodded. "True enough. I was petrified of you then."

He cocked an eyebrow at her statement. "And now?"

She stepped into Mica's arms. "Now I have Mica—and I've been around vampires for a little while now." She shrugged. "I don't know. It's just different now."

"Come on, Desiree. Let's go get something to eat," Sherry said urgently. She gave Drake and Mica an uneasy glance, then looked back at Desiree pointedly. "I'm starving."

Desiree looked up at Mica and smiled. "We'll be back in an hour or so."

He kissed her forehead gently. "I'll be waiting."

Drake crossed his arms over his chest. "I'll be waiting too."

He'll be waiting for me, ran through Sherry's mind, causing a warmth to flutter through her heart. Her steps faltered with the sudden urge to run back and throw herself into his arms. *Slow down girl, he's not here waiting for you, he's here to see Desiree, remember?* Her mind screamed at her. *Besides, he's not for you. He's a vampire. Witches and vampires don't mix. Don't go and do something stupid to embarrass yourself all over again. Just get the hell out of here and try to salvage what's left of your dignity. Put one foot in front of the other and just walk out that door. Now!* She clutched Desiree's jacket sleeve and tugged. "Come on— please."

"Charles is out front waiting in the limo," Mica remarked. "He'll drive you both wherever you need to go."

Desiree stopped in mid-step, then turned back to Mica in surprise. "You have a limo?"

Mica smiled and winked at her. "Yes, *we* do. How were you intending on getting to the restaurant?"

She shrugged. "I thought we would go in Sherry's car."

Mica shook his head. "You need a bodyguard."

"But—"

He let out a slow breath and continued to shake his head. "After everything that happened last week, you're not going anywhere by yourself. I don't want to go through any of that again."

"But—"

"Desiree, this isn't up for debate."

"Fine," she said through clenched teeth. "Come on Sherry, let's go find our babysitter."

Drake roared with laughter. "Are you having trouble in paradise already?"

Desiree straightened her shoulders and marched out of the house with Sherry in tow. She slammed the door behind her. "Of all the arrogant, egotistical...."

Sherry laughed softly. "Drake shouldn't have laughed, but Mica's right." She shook her head and climbed into the backseat of the limo. "You shouldn't call Mica names like that. You were almost killed several times last week. He's just trying to protect you."

Desiree's eyebrow shot up. "I was referring to Drake with my comments," she huffed.

Sherry's mouth dropped open. "Drake? He didn't do anything. Mica was the one bossing you around, not Drake."

Desiree shot her a suspicious look. "Hummmm...."

"And that's supposed to mean—what?"

Desiree settled into the seat across from Sherry. "You and I need to have a serious talk, girlfriend."

Karen Fuller

Chapter Five

Sherry pushed her plate away and leaned back in the booth. "Okay, Desiree, now that my stomach is no longer touching my backbone, I'd like you to finish your story. I have nothing against your boyfriend, but I'd like to hear the rest of this story without any interruptions."

Desiree gave her a blank look. "So much has happened that I can't remember where I left off."

Sherry rolled her eyes and grinned. "You were about to tell me what happened after the vampires carted the others off."

"Okay, when the other vampire clan carted the others off, they left me in that dark cave by myself." The smile dropped from Desiree's face, and she shook her head. "I never really knew that I was afraid of the dark until the trip to that cave." She shivered. "Anyway, I swallowed my fear and made my way outside to the van. I knew Mica had left the cell phone there. My plan was to call Drake and get help." Sherry sat up and listened more attentively. "Anyway, I called Drake, and unfortunately there was no way that any of them could get from New Orleans to Sevierville before sunup. Drake had suggested that I let Mica get himself out of his predicament, and that I needed to come back to New Orleans."

35

Sherry tilted her head in confusion. "But—he didn't want to help? I don't understand. You were there because of him."

"No, I was there because Jason Hargrove kidnapped me and carted me off to Salem. Drake sent Mica to rescue me, and—well—it's not that he didn't want to help…I think that if we had been close enough, he would have sent a rescue party." She shrugged. "I guess he figured that Mica and Denise weren't going to make it, and he really wanted that spell." She rolled her eyes and shrugged again. "Anyway, I told him that I wasn't coming back to New Orleans without Mica. He said that he was sorry, but there was no time for them to get there, and that I was on my own for the rescue."

"So, if Drake didn't send you any help, then how did they get away?"

"You see, Mica and I have bonded as mates. We can feel what each other feels. I discovered through that bond that I can communicate with him as well. He allowed me to see through his eyes, so that I could see where they were." She shrugged. "I cast a couple of spells, one of which was for the keys to the Express Van. They really weren't that far away, just a few miles. I parked the van at a safe distance and snuck up on the vampires." She bit her lip apprehensively. "I cast a spell so that the vampire clan would think that they were seeing the light of day, and that they would feel the burn of the sun's rays, and the only way to get away from the burn was to hide in the shadows until my task was done. They scattered to the caves to hide."

Sherry laughed. "That was brilliant!"

Desiree smiled sheepishly. "I thought so too, but Mica was mad as hell."

"You saved his butt, didn't you?"

She nodded. "Yeah, but that wasn't the problem. Mica was afraid that by me casting that spell, the clan of vampires would seek me out to kill me for revenge."

Sherry swallowed hard. "That would be bad. I guess that's why you have the bodyguard now, huh?"

She shook her head. "No—not really…the clan found us last night at Drake's headquarters. They wouldn't listen to reason and attacked all of us. They're all dead now."

"Okay—so—why does Mica think you need a bodyguard?"

She shrugged. "I think he might be a little over protective…I couldn't imagine who else could be after me. But then again, this time last week I didn't know all this would happen, either."

The waitress brought a pot of coffee to the table, along with the check. "Would y'all care for more coffee?"

Desiree held out her cup. "Yes, please."

Sherry smiled up at the waitress. "I would love another cup."

The waitress filled their cups, and both women picked up their cups and took a sip.

Sherry placed the mug on the table, cradling it in her hands. "So, it sounds like you had quite an adventure."

"Yeah, I did. Things were a little scary at times, but I really don't have many regrets from it."

Desiree's tone had Sherry tilting her head and staring hard at her friend. "You have some regrets? Aren't you happy that you're with Mica?"

Desiree sighed heavily. "Oh, I'm very happy that I wound up with Mica. The last ninety years have been very lonely for me, and he makes me feel again."

Sherry smirked. "I bet he does."

Desiree cleared her throat and smiled. "Yes, well—he does at that, but that's not what I meant." She laughed lightly, then picked up her coffee cup and took another sip. "I meant emotionally. I now feel a purpose that I haven't felt in years. Mica's the best thing that has ever happened to me."

"So, if Mica's the best thing that has ever happened to you, then what's the regret?"

Desiree's gaze leveled with hers. "I regret the loss of my freedom."

"I'm sure this thing with the bodyguard won't last long, and then Mica should let you do what you want."

"It's not Mica holding me captive." Her eyes dropped to the coffee cup. "Drake is my captor, not Mica."

Sherry sat back in her seat, then threw out her hand. "How can *Drake* be your captor?"

Desiree looked up, then shrugged. "He is the king of this area, and what he says is law. It took a lot of fast-talking to get Drake to relent and let me leave his protection to stay with Mica. If I refuse to do what he says, he will command me to move back into the warehouse, and I will have no choice. Since Mica and I are mates, he will allow Mica to come with me, but Mica doesn't like living with the nest. I couldn't do that to him. So, I do as I'm told."

"But—but—that's just not fair."

"Whether it's fair or not is irrelevant. Drake is a dangerous man with a hot temper, and is accustomed to getting *everything* he wants. Those that oppose him have a very short life span. He doesn't handle the word '*no*' very well either." She sighed. "Since I was able to cast that spell for him, he thinks of me as a valuable possession. He told us that there's a vampire war brewing, and a clan about three times the size of Drakes is vying for his territory. He thinks my magic can help, and only allows me to leave as long as I remain at his beck and call." She brought a trembling hand up to her forehead. "Hey, is it me, or is it getting warm in here?"

Sherry shifted uneasily in her seat and pulled on the collar of her sweater. "It is a little warm in here."

"It must be my lack of sleep, but I'm getting overwhelmingly tired."

"Now that you mention it, I'm extremely tired too."

Desiree took a twenty out of her purse and placed it on the table with the check. "I need to run to the lady's room and splash some cold water on my face before we leave. Maybe it'll help."

"I'll go with you." They each grabbed their purses. "Are we going straight back to the mansion?" They slid out of the booth and made their way to the lady's room.

"That was the plan."

"I guess we'll talk about the coven stuff when we get back to your house then."

Desiree sighed heavily. "I may have to give you a rain check for a couple of hours on that one. I think I need to lie down."

"Are you really that tired?" Sherry asked as she opened the door to the lady's room.

Desiree brushed past her and headed straight for the sink. "I'm afraid so." She ran the cold water and splashed it on her face, then grabbed a paper towel, wet it, and placed it on the back of her neck.

"Desiree, you don't look so hot. Maybe I need to call Mica."

Desiree stood up straight at the mention of calling Mica. "No! I'm just tired—I'll be okay." She swayed a little on her feet and grabbed the edge of the sink. "Just give me a minute."

"You look like you're going to pass out. Sit down on the floor and put your head between your knees."

Desiree shook her head. "No—I'll be...." Desiree's eyes rolled in the back of her head, then she hit the ceramic tile floor of the bathroom.

Sherry hit her knees on the floor next to her friend's unconscious body. She grabbed her shoulders and shook her. "Desiree...Desiree...wake up! Something's wrong with you, and we need to get out of here!" She brought a trembling hand to her own forehead as her head started to swim too. Her heart raced with fear. "Oh God, I think we've been drugged. Please—wake—up...." She fell forward, unconscious, across Desiree.

***

A lone figure opened the bathroom stall and stood over the girls' unconscious bodies. He pushed on Desiree's shoulder with the toe of his boot. She didn't budge. "Let's see you get away again, witch," he growled.

Chapter Six

Drake paced the floor impatiently. How long could it possibly take to eat breakfast? He looked up at the clock on the mantel. "What's taking them so long?"

Mica's patience with Drake was sorely tested, and he couldn't hide the irritation in his voice. "Wearing a hole in my carpet isn't going to make them return any faster. Please sit down."

"I'll sit down when I'm damn good and ready to sit down, and not a minute before."

Mica really didn't want to argue with him, but Drake's agitation was getting on Mica's nerves. Desiree was *his* mate, and he didn't like her at Drake's every beck and call. He sighed heavily. "I can feel Desiree's moods; she won't run, if that's what you're worried about. She might not like being under your royal thumb, but she won't leave me. Besides, I've sent Charles with them. He'll keep an eye on her. Desiree should be safe enough."

Drake stopped in mid-stride and turned on his friend. "I wasn't referring to Desiree," he snarled impatiently. "She's your mate. Of course she'll come back...you are bonded to each other. Sherry, on the other hand, might not be so compelled to come back. She might choose to take this opportunity to run, and I won't stand for it. *I* want *her* back."

41

Mica's unexpected laughter didn't set well with Drake. "I don't see what is so funny about the possibility of Sherry running."

"Do you hear yourself? You won't stand for it? Last time I checked, she didn't have to answer to you. She is not one of your subjects that has to jump at *your* every order and do what *you* say, when *you* say it. She—" The laughter was directly cut off, and he drew his eyebrows together in a frown, swaying in his seat. "What in the...?"

"You were saying?" Drake remarked dryly.

Mica closed his eyes and braced his hands to steady himself. "Something has happened to Desiree. I can feel it."

Drake's irritation was replaced with concern. "What do you mean? What do you feel?"

Mica opened his eyes, staring into space; he was searching for his connection with Desiree. "It feels so— strange. I felt her get dizzy all of a sudden...and then...nothing." He shook himself, then looked back at his friend. "She must be unconscious, because I feel nothing."

"Try harder," Drake demanded.

Mica closed his eyes again and tried to seek Desiree out. He held his mouth in a tight, grim line in concentration. He opened his eyes, shook his head, and then looked up at his friend in alarm. "Nothing—I see nothing. When I try to see through her eyes, all I see is a black void. She's either in a dark place, or she's unconscious. Since I don't feel any fear, I have to assume that she's unconscious."

Drake's agitation increased and he paced faster as he tried to think of a logical solution. "Does your driver carry a cell phone?" Mica nodded. "Well, what are you waiting for? Call him!"

Mica reached for the phone and called his driver. He didn't even give Charles a chance to say "hello". "Where is Desiree?" he demanded into the receiver.

"Huh? They're at the table—uh—they were at the table."

Mica closed his eyes and ground his teeth. His anger barely held in check. "What do you mean *were*?"

"Were!" Drake barked, then grabbed the phone from his friend. "There better be a good explanation for your statement," he growled coldly into the receiver.

"I don't know," Charles said nervously. "I saw the waitress give them more coffee and hand them the check. I—uh—assumed that they'd be right out once they finished their coffee." He swallowed hard. "I didn't see them get up from the table."

Drake clenched his teeth and growled into the receiver. "If you value your life, you'll go inside and find them."

***

Charles looked at the phone in his hand and felt the blood drain from his face. His hands shook, and he couldn't hide the tremor of fear in his voice. "Uh—yes sir—uh—I mean—sire. I'll do that right now." He scrambled out of the limo and hurried into the diner. His eyes darted frantically around the room. His heart sank. They weren't there. "I—uh...." He cleared his throat. "I don't see them, sire."

"What?"

"Hang on a second," Charles said nervously. He palmed the phone in one hand to muffle the sound, rushed over to the waitress, and grabbed her by the arm with his free hand. She whipped her head around in alarm. She looked from his frightened eyes down to his hand gripping her arm, and then back up into his eyes again. "Excuse me, miss." He pointed to the empty table. "Where did those ladies go?"

She shrugged. "They left a few minutes ago. The brunette left the money and tip on the table." She shook her head in thought. "I didn't see where they went. Is there a problem?"

He closed his eyes and nodded frantically. "Yeah, there's a problem. Please think hard. My life depends on it."

She chewed on her thumbnail in thought, and then she shook her head again. "I'm sorry, but I didn't see anything. If you didn't see them leave, then maybe they're in the lady's room."

"Could you please check for me? That's the one place I can't go."

She nodded. "Sure, I'll check, but you're going to have to let go of my arm first."

He let go. "Sorry."

"No problem. I'll be right back." She walked toward the lady's room, and rubbed the red mark left behind from his grip as she walked.

He put the phone back up to his ear. "Uh, I have the waitress checking the lady's room."

"They better be there."

He watched her walk inside, and then come back out shaking her head. "The room is empty."

"No, it can't be," he said in a panic. He rushed past her, threw the door open wide, and charged inside.

She was right on his heels. "Sir, you can't go in there," she said urgently.

He spun around the room in a circle, and his frightened eyes scanned every crevice looking for any sign of the women. The room was empty, just like the waitress said. His heart sank, and a feeling of dread washed over him. He walked back out of the room and left the waitress standing at the open door. He leaned against the wall and brought the phone back up to his ear. His hands were visibly shaking, and he hung his head in defeat. "I'm sorry, sire, they're gone."

Charles heard the receiver of the phone crack in Drake's grip. "Don't move." His voice held a deadly edge. "Mica and I will be there momentarily."

Charles snapped the cell phone shut, and it dropped from his numbed fingers to the carpeted floor. His legs turned to rubber and would no longer support his weight. He slid down the wall to a sitting position on the floor, and stared vacantly into the crowded restaurant. He swallowed hard. "I'm a dead man," he mumbled to himself. "What was I thinking, going to work for a vampire? I'll tell ya what you were thinking, you dumb ass; you were thinking that this would be a cushy job and easy money. All ya had to do was drive their ladies to get something to eat, keep an eye on them, and make sure that they stayed safe. It should have been a piece of cake, just a simple, easy job. Any moron off the street should have been able to handle those orders, but you had to get bored and read a book instead of doing your job. Now those vamps are going to rip your throat out and drain you dry." He propped his elbows on his knees and dropped his face into his shaking hands in dejection.

The waitress knelt down and placed her hand on his shoulder in concern. "Are you going to be okay? You don't look well at all." She chewed on her bottom lip, unsure how to help him. "Do I need to call someone for you?"

He looked up at her and leaned his head back on the wall behind him. He shook his head and swallowed hard to find his voice. "In a little while, I won't have anything left to worry about." His voice held an ominous note. "Someone's already coming for me."

Karen Fuller

Chapter Seven

Drake slung the broken phone down on the table in anger. He couldn't stand incompetence, and now Sherry's life was in danger as a result. A deep rage consumed him, and he stormed toward the front door. "What other transportation do you have other than that limo?" he growled at Mica.

"Stop, you're heading the wrong way. The Rolls Phantom is in the garage, and the garage is around back." Mica headed for the garage with Drake hot on his heels. He took the keys from the peg by the back door, then hit the button for the garage door opener as he was climbing behind the wheel. Drake slid into the passenger seat and slammed the door. Mica could feel his friend's anger and anxiety. He felt it himself. "We'll find them."

Drake's jaw clenched and his eyes held a steely glare. "We'd better find them. If we don't, your driver had better pray for a quick death."

"You'll have to stand in line." Mica put the key into the ignition and the engine roared to life. He punched the gas pedal. The tires squealed and then caught, leaving a black streak of rubber on the polished floor. He pulled out of the driveway on two wheels.

***

The diner was just a few blocks away, and he squealed the tires again as he took the corner into the parking lot. Mica pulled in and parked next to his limo. They both jumped out and stormed toward the diner.

Charles looked up when he heard the front door open, and then he saw them storm through the door like two avenging gods. He had never felt as much fear in his life. He swallowed hard and struggled to his feet. He bowed his head. "Mica...Drake...I...I'm...."

Mica grabbed him by the collar, suspended him in mid-air, then shoved him hard up against the wall. "Save it!" he snarled, and most of the patrons stopped eating to gawk their way.

Charles lifted his eyes to meet Mica's, and what he saw in those eyes petrified him. He saw a primal hunger with a thirst for vengeance, and no leniency. That steely gaze held a promise of a painful death. "Don't move a muscle." Mica put Charles back down on his feet, then brushed past him, heading straight for the women's bathroom.

Drake took over where Mica left off and gripped the frightened driver's arm in his steely grasp. He whispered viciously in his ear. "If your incompetence has resulted in harm coming to *my woman*, you better pray for a quick death, because I will enjoy making you suffer."

Charles was sure that the king had just sentenced him to death, and the remaining color drained from his face. He kept his mouth shut, because he knew any apologies or excuses would fall on deaf ears. He closed his eyes and hung his head.

***

The waitress was hot on Mica's heels. "Sir! You can't go—" Her eyes grew wide and the words froze on her lips when he turned his icy glare on her. "Uh—I mean...." She backed away in a hurry. "Never mind." She turned away and ran into the kitchen.

He snatched the door off its hinges in his haste. Desiree's scent was stronger in this room than anywhere else. His eyes darted around the room looking for clues, and that's when he caught another scent. It was vaguely familiar, but not quite the same. His eyes narrowed when he identified the scent. *That's impossible, there is no way that spell could be broken.* "Hargrove...," he growled.

He stormed out of the women's bathroom and locked eyes with Drake. "We have to go back to the warehouse. I don't know how he's managed it, but Hargrove is behind this."

"He can't be, unless Desiree's spell has been broken."

"His scent is strong in that bathroom, and mixed with Desiree's. There's something a little off about the scent, and I can't quite detect exactly what it is. Maybe her spell caused it to alter a little, but I'd recognize that stench anywhere. We've got to hurry. He wants Desiree dead, and since he's a witch hunter I'm sure he'll target Sherry too."

Drake yanked on Charles's arm. "We've got to get this one back to the warehouse and put under guard, and then we'll plan our next move."

Mica nodded and grabbed Charles's other arm, and together they hauled him out of the restaurant. Mica opened the back door to the Phantom and shoved Charles into the backseat. Both Mica and Drake lifted their heads to the sounds of sirens heading their way. They didn't have time to deal with the police at the moment. They exchanged a quick glance, then got in the car and sped out of the parking lot in the direction of the warehouse.

Mica parked the Phantom around back, and they hauled Charles into the building. Sean met them at the door, and he couldn't hide his surprise at finding Mica at the door with Drake. His eyes darted between the two, then centered on the human dangling in their grip. Sean opened his mouth to speak, but when Drake raised an eyebrow at him, he shut his mouth again and waited.

"Has anyone called in with any demands?" Drake barked.

"Demands?" He shook his head. "No. No one has called. What's going on?"

"Desiree and Sherry have been snatched." He glared hard at Sean. "Tell me how it is that you let Hargrove escape from here?" he growled.

His eyes grew wide at the accusation. "Hargrove has escaped?" He frowned and shook his head. "That's impossible. He's in a cage in your chambers, sire. He wouldn't have been able to leave without our notice."

He raised an eyebrow. "Then please explain to me how his scent is all over the place where Desiree was nabbed."

He shook his head again. "I can't, but can I assure you that he hasn't left this building."

Drake glanced over at Mica. "Let's go see for ourselves if Hargrove is or isn't in my chambers." He turned his head and glared back at Sean. "For your sake, he'd better be there."

A hint of anxiety passed over Sean's features, and then his confidence returned. "He'll be there, sire."

"He had better be!" he thundered, and then he yanked on Charles's arm and headed for his chamber. When he got there he threw open the door with a force that bounced the heavy door off the wall. His eyes went immediately to the fireplace, and there, sitting on the mantle, was the cage containing Jason Hargrove. He was still a rat, and therefore not capable of kidnapping the women.

Mica let go of Charles's arm, stormed to the fireplace, and snatched the cage off of the mantle, and the rat inside squealed in terror. He shoved the cage back on top of the mantle in agitation. "That was Hargrove's scent. We've been dealing with him for days. I know that scent. Does he have any children?"

Sean scoffed. "Why would it matter if the human had any children?"

"I now know why Drake keeps you locked up in here," Mica growled at Sean. "If he has a child then the DNA would be similar. It might explain the similarities in scent. It appears that our rat here may have an offspring—but not for long!" He stormed out of Drake's chamber.

Drake shoved Charles toward Sean. "Lock him up."

"What did the human do?"

"He was careless enough to lose our women," he growled.

Sean cocked his head to the side and raised an eyebrow in question. "Women?"

The look on Drake's face was grim at Sean's question. He nodded. "Yes, it appears that I may have found myself a woman—that is if I can keep her alive long enough."

"Mica sure is bold bringing other female vampires around his mate." Sean grinned at the prospect of a fight between Mica and his mate. "His witch wasn't jealous?"

Drake shook his head. "What are you babbling about?"

"Desiree, his witch—wasn't she jealous of his female friends?" Sean wiggled his eyebrows.

"Sherry is Desiree's friend, not Mica's, and she has absolutely nothing to be jealous about."

The disappointment was clear on Sean's face. "Still, for some unknown reason, women find him irresistible. Human or vampire, I would think that she would be protective of her mate."

"She is a witch like Desiree, and she shows no interest in Mica." He smiled. "She showed an interest in me from the time I walked through Mica's door. Yes, I look forward to getting to know that one much better."

Sean's mouth went slack with that news. He had seen what Desiree did to Hargrove, and he wasn't happy with the prospect that another witch might be hanging around the nest. "She's a witch? I had assumed that this woman was another vampire…you know, immortal, like us."

"Oh, I've already given Desiree the order to make her immortal."

"She must be a brave woman to allow another witch to cast an immortality spell on her."

Drake raised an eyebrow. "I gave an order, not a choice."

Sean barked with laughter. "I bet that order went well."

He furrowed his brow. "No, not really—but it doesn't matter. I am king, and what I say goes."

Sean laughed harder. "A take charge attitude with strong willed women. Good luck with that one."

Drake narrowed his eyes and growled. "I am king, and they wouldn't dare disobey—"

Mica rushed back into the room and interrupted Drake's tirade. "Desiree's awake, and I know where they are."

"They're both alive?"

"She said that they were, but she's tied up and that son of a bitch is threatening to kill them. We have to hurry."

Drake nodded, then turned to Charles. "You may yet live, human," he growled, and then he looked up at Sean. "Now, lock him up until we return."

Sean bowed his head. "Yes, sire."

Chapter Eight

Sherry moaned as she slowly gained consciousness and brought her trembling hand up to her temple. She had a splitting headache. Her fogged mind also noted that she was lying down in cramped quarters. The air was hot and stuffy, making it difficult to breathe. Muffled, angry voices could be heard from the other side of the wall that surrounded her. She strained her ears to listen.

Her ears picked up the taunting of an unidentified male voice. "You're not so high and mighty now, are ya witch?"

"I know who you are—you—you son-of-a-bitch! You better let me and my friend go, or I'll make you very sorry!" Sherry decided that it was definitely Desiree yelling at the unknown man.

***

Desiree struggled against her bonds. *Mica, we're in trouble.*

Where are you?

Desiree glanced around the room. *I don't know for sure. It looks like a mausoleum.*

Who did this? I thought I recognized Hargrove's scent, but he's still in the cage at Drake's lair.

Desiree yanked on her bonds again, glaring at her captor. *It's that little worm's son, Justin.*

Are you two okay?
For now.
Stall him, we're on our way.

Desiree yanked again, then screamed out her frustration. "If you value your life, you had better let us go, asshole."

Justin walked up to her, taking her chin between his fingers, forcing her to look at him. "Tisk... tisk...you have such foul language coming out of that pretty mouth. Maybe I'll decide to take my pleasure from you before I do away with you."

Desiree tried to yank her chin out of his grip. "If you try it, I'll take great pleasure in cutting out your heart and feeding it back to you," she spat, and then she laughed tauntingly. "No, I'll take that back. Go ahead and try it. Mica will eat your heart for lunch, saving me the trouble."

Jason let go of her chin, placing his hands on his hips. He chuckled. "You are a liar. My daddy and I have been watching you for years. You don't have a protector." He reached out, grabbed a hand full of her hair, and yanked her face close to his, close enough for her to smell his foul breath. "You're just a hundred and twenty-five year old witch that will soon be bound to the stake and burned for her crimes."

Desiree laughed at his assumptions, and then she spit in his face. He let go of her hair and backhanded her across the face, then he reached up and wiped the spittle from his cheek.

Her senses reeled and she tasted blood, but it wasn't in her nature to give up, especially since he was just as easy to goad as his father. She narrowed her eyes and grinned spitefully at him through of her swollen, blood stained lips. "Mica felt that, and he's going to make you pay for that, Justin Hargrove. Maybe I'll just do to you what I did to your daddy," she goaded him.

"You're lying; there is no Mica, and you ain't done nothin' to my daddy."

***

"Justin Hargrove," Sherry whispered to herself. "Did Desiree mention the name Hargrove to me this morning?" Her heart sank as the realization struck her. "Oh God, he's a witch hunter." The situation out there was getting way out of hand. She decided it was time to get out of her confinement. But what was she confined in? It was so dark and stuffy. She inched her hands out in front of her and felt around, and what she felt was silk or maybe satin. She froze when the realization struck her: her heart slammed frantically in her chest, and then her hands sought madly around. A scream of terror erupted from her throat. It was ear piercing inside of the coffin, but could only be heard as a muffled sound outside of it. She beat the lid hysterically with her fists and feet. Her fingers tore at the lining, shredding it with her sharp fingernails. Her terror was fueled further by her over active imagination.

"Sherry!" Desiree shouted. "Calm down! Mica and Drake are on their way." Desiree fought her bindings.

Desiree's words barely registered to Sherry. "I want out!"

Justin laughed gleefully at Sherry's distress, and then he slammed his hand down on top of the coffin a couple of times to irritate her. "Desiree lies, there's no one coming to your rescue. No one knows that you both are here. No one pays much attention to a hearse in a cemetery, or a man unloading coffins into a mausoleum. It was a perfect set up, and if anybody was looking for you, they would never think to look for dead bodies in a crypt. I'm a genius," he ranted self-righteously. "Once I take care of your friend, then I'll deal with you too, witch."

"Someone please help us!" Sherry shouted from the top of her lungs.

"Give it up, witch," Justin taunted gleefully.

***

The heavy vault doors burst open and bounced against the walls with such force they fell off their hinges. Justin gasped in shocked fear as two giant men rushed through the opening.

Desiree's face split into a wide grin through her swollen, blood-crusted lips. "Mica!"

Mica's eyes lit on her face in relief that she was still alive, and then he took in the condition of her battered face. He growled as his eyes trained in on Justin. He wanted vengeance for his abused mate.

Justin turned to run, but there was nowhere to go. The vampires blocked the only exit. Suddenly his perfect plan didn't seem so smart. He held up his hands in front of him defensively. "Uh—gentlemen—I'm…." He swallowed hard. "I'm…s-s-sorry," he stuttered, and then he backed into the wall. He couldn't retreat any further. He hit his knees and cowered away from Mica. "I thought she was lying." His voice was weak with fear. "Out of all the years that we've watched her and waited, she's never had a boyfriend before."

Mica reached down, grabbed Justin by the throat, and suspended him in mid-air. "You laid your hands on my mate, and for that you will suffer," he growled.

Justin trembled from head to toe, and frantically clawed at the fingers wrapped around his neck. His bladder let go in his fear. Mica shook his head in disgust at the coward he held at bay in his hand. Justin choked and lost consciousness, and Mica dropped his lifeless body to the floor.

Drake anxiously looked around the room for Sherry. "Where is she?" he growled at the unconscious body on the floor. He turned his head and glared at Mica, and pointed at

Justin. "You should have made him produce Sherry before you choked him."

Mica shook his head and rushed over to Desiree to untie her. She smiled up at him as he reached for her bindings. "You came for me." Relief rang clear in her voice.

He smiled and looked deeply into her eyes. "Did you ever doubt me?"

She threw her now free hands around his neck. "Never!" she said enthusiastically and kissed him soundly.

"Help!"

Drake turned and looked all around the room for the source of Sherry's voice.

"Drake, Sherry's still locked in the coffin," Desiree said urgently, and then Sherry kicked the lid of the coffin for good measure.

Drake ripped the lid off, throwing it in the corner. Sherry shielded her eyes from the sudden light, and drew in big gulps of fresh air. He took her hand and pulled it away from her face so he could look at her and see for himself that she was unharmed. Their eyes met, she was suddenly lost in his startling blue eyes, and her heart raced as the heat of his gaze washed over her. "Thank you," she said timidly. "I was almost out of air in there." She propped up on her elbows, looking around to take in her surroundings. She had a sudden chill; crypts weren't exactly on her list of top places to wake up in. On the scan back around the room her eyes caught Desiree's gaze, and she flushed deeply. She knew that Desiree was concerned with Drake's sudden interest in her, and something in the back of her mind told her that she should be too, but at the current moment, she just didn't care to fight it. She looked back up at him. "Could you please help me get out of this thing? I still feel the effects of the drug, and I don't know if I can manage to get out on my own."

***

Desiree gripped Mica's arm in shock when she saw the heated looks exchanged between Drake and Sherry. She was afraid for her friend, and she had every intention of charging over to the coffin and checking on Sherry herself. Mica held her back and silently shook his head.

***

Drake heard the change in Sherry's heartbeat as soon as their eyes met, and his keen sense of smell caught her subtle change in scent. He smiled, knowing the effect he had on her and her on him…it was a tangible thing. Her allure was undeniable, and he felt very protective of her. He didn't know why this witch intrigued him as much as she did, but he had every intention of finding out. He hadn't felt a yearning this strong in over a hundred years. He was king; he was used to women swooning at his feet and freely offering themselves to him for his pleasure. She was different, and he wanted her. No, he had to have her.

***

Their eyes met again, and she caught her breath at the intensity of his gaze. She felt the heat rush through her body, leaving her moist and aching in response. He reached inside the coffin, her skin tingling at the surprisingly tender touch of his fingers as he slid them beneath her and lifted her gently out. She slipped her trembling arms around his neck to steady herself and felt the silky texture of his long hair, and couldn't resist the temptation to run her fingers through it. She had fully expected him to set her back down on her feet, but he held her tightly in his arms against his rock hard chest instead. She tried to move and her overly sensitive nipples beaded as they rubbed against his chest. Her eyes widened in surprise as this sensation sent a fiery jolt straight to her core. His nearness alone was playing havoc on her senses, and she couldn't remember ever wanting something so much in her life. No one had ever made her feel that strongly before.

He inched his face toward hers, and she moistened her dry lips in anticipation. His lips gently met hers, and her body trembled with a sudden need to seek more. She wanted to taste what those sweet lips offered as fire coursed through her veins with the sensation. A simple kiss had never had this kind of effect on her before. She parted her lips and moaned as his tongue sought hers.

She entwined her fingers in the hair at the base of his neck, pulling him closer, deepening the kiss. The fingers on her other hand worked the top buttons of his shirt, then slipped beneath the fabric to caress his smooth skin.

This triggered an approving growl from him as he broke the kiss. "Hold onto me." He shifted his hold so that she could wrap her legs around his waist. Using his free hand, he cupped her breast, rubbing her sensitized nipple through the fabric.

The huskiness of his voice sent a ripple of pleasure through her and his touch was driving her mad. Her lips followed the path of her fingers, pushing the fabric away. She kissed and nipped at his flesh as she trailed a path to his nipple. He rocked his hips against her soft core as she took the round disk between her teeth and gently bit then suckled the wound.

"Sherry!"

The shock in Desiree's voice brought her back to her senses. What was she thinking? She had never behaved this way with anyone before. She heard Mica chuckle in the background. Her eyes flew open and she reluctantly pushed away. She felt the heat rise to her face, remembering the way she had just reacted to him.

When she looked up, he was smiling, looking down at her. His fangs had dropped and his eyes held an unnatural glow. The look in his eyes promised long nights of hot passion, and her body was reacting to the open invitation, both reminding her that she was dealing with a vampire and treading on very dangerous territory.

She took a quivering breath, then spoke. "Please put me down."

Drake laughed softly as he complied, setting her on her feet. Her legs still felt wobbly and she clutched his arm to remain steady.

"Thank you," she mumbled. She looked around the room, then shivered. The light from the doorway flooded the interior, allowing Sherry to clearly see her surroundings. She wrinkled her nose at the smell. The room was dank and musty. Water droplets trickled down the walls. Three pedestals held coffins in the center. Two benches lined the walls, one of which was occupied by Desiree and Mica. Her gaze stopped on Desiree. "You both saw that, didn't you?"

Desiree nodded. "Yeah, kiddo—are you okay?"

Sherry shrugged. "Yeah, I guess. Waking up in a coffin probably took about ten years off my life."

"Yeah, I imagine that would be scary, but I was referring to just now."

Drake frowned at Desiree, and Sherry unconsciously stepped back, bumping into Drake. He wrapped his arms possessively around her, alarming Desiree further.

Sherry shook her head. "Desiree, I'm fine. It was just a kiss."

"It looked like more than a kiss to me." She stood, then gripped Sherry's shoulders. "You're playing with fire." She shook her to stress her point then shoved her toward the door. "Run!"

Drake tucked Sherry behind him. "Mica, control your mate!"

Desiree slammed her hands on her hips and yelled into Drake's face. "I told you that you can't have my friend."

"I am king!" he roared. "You are one of my subjects and have no say in who I see or don't see. I can have anyone I please."

She crossed her arms over her chest. "Not Sherry!"

Mica gripped Desiree's shoulders, pulling her back. "Desiree, enough."

"But, Mica—"

"Love, she is a grown woman and capable of making her own decisions."

"Mica, I watched her grow up. I taught her the craft—you don't understand. She is like a daughter to me—I have to protect her."

Sherry stepped from behind Drake and stood next to him. "Desiree, I've been taking care of myself for quite a few years now—"

Desiree smiled sadly and interjected. "I know. I also know I have no rights or control over your life. But Drake is—"

"Is what?" She cut in, losing her temper. "Strong, handsome, too good for me maybe?"

Desiree shook her head. "No, that's not what I meant...you didn't let me finish."

Sherry crossed her arms over her chest and continued to glare at Desiree. "By all means, finish, *Mom*. You won't be happy until you do."

"Sherry, please, don't be that way."

"I asked you to finish."

"Very well, I'll finish. I was going to say that Drake is dangerous."

Sherry nodded. "And Mica's not?"

Desiree was taken aback by that question. "I—"

Drake roared with laughter and clapped his hands. "Touché!"

Desiree huffed. "I don't find this the least bit amusing, Drake. She has no idea what she's getting herself into. She's—"

"Desiree, you are my very best friend, and I love you, but if you're going to say that I'm naïve, then you'd better not finish that sentence."

Desiree threw up her hands and looked away. "Fine, you're obviously not ready to listen to reas...." Her eyes widened and the color drained from her face. "Good God!"

Mica turned her to face him. "I felt that...you're trembling and afraid." Mica searched her face. "And pale. What just happened?"

Her eyes watered and a few tears rolled down her cheeks. She closed her eyes and spoke to him in a whisper. "Hargrove's gone."

Mica's eyes glowed red as his focus zoomed in on the corner. In the blink of an eye he had tucked Desiree protectively behind him, his fangs dropping as he assumed a fighting stance.

Sherry screamed, stumbling backwards into a coffin, knocking it from the pedestal with a resounding crash. Drake snatched her up before she could hit the floor. His eyes too were glowing red, and his fangs exposed. She screamed again, struggling to get away, sure that her life was about to come to an end. "Let me go."

"Stop fighting me. I have to protect you."

"*What?*"

"Hargrove's gone."

Dangerous

Chapter Nine

Sherry stopped struggling, then strained to see past Drake into the darkened corner of the room. "Wh-where'd he go?"

Drake set her back down on her feet, but kept her close. He glared at Desiree. "My guess is he slipped out while Desiree was arguing with us."

Desiree's shoulders slumped. "I guess it was bad timing. I still don't think—"

A growl rumbled from Drake's chest. "Mica…."

Mica covered Desiree's mouth before she could finish her sentence, and she struggled against his grip. "Desiree, please. You haven't learned all our ways yet. We are a warrior clan, as you know. Obedience is a must. If you persist, Drake could order me to punish you—I would have no choice." She froze.

Sherry brought a trembling hand up to cover her mouth, giving Drake an uneasy glance as she asked, "What's the punishment for disobedience?"

Drake didn't take his eyes off Desiree as he spoke. "A public flogging." Desiree's eyes rounded. "In most instances the punishment is carried out by the one wronged, or the leader whose orders have been disobeyed. With the threat of this type of punishment there is very little disobedience. Orders are followed without question. But in Desiree's case the one wielding the whip would be her mate, Mica. A vampire is not allowed to harm another's mate, so the mate is ordered to carry out the punishment. If the mate refuses to administer punishment, then they are both put to death."

Sherry gripped Drake's arm and shook her head frantically. "No, Drake, please don't—"

Drake placed his hand over hers. "She has tested my patience, little one."

"Please?"

"I have already been more lenient with her than any of my other subjects. I am grateful for what she has done for me and my kind. Granting us the ability to walk in the daylight gives us the capability of blending in with humans, and an advantage over other clans. But as a leader, my orders must be followed by my people without question. I am not a cruel master, but I do demand obedience. Mica is my best friend and her mate. I sired Mica three hundred years ago, and through that bond I can feel what he feels for your friend. They are soul mates. Vampires are fiercely loyal and protect their mates with their life. Through their bond Mica would feel every stroke of the whip as it rent through her flesh, and each strike would tear at his heart. I, in turn, would feel *his* pain through our bond. I do not wish to cause her harm, but if she slips and is defiant in front of others, I will have no choice but to demand punishment or my clan would perceive my lack of reaction a weakness. That, I cannot allow."

***

Mica whispered in Desiree's ear. "Now do you understand why I keep intervening? I know the consequences of your actions. I have seen the results. You remember Denise; she crossed Drake a time or two. Her smart mouth has been known to test a man's temper. One day she pushed Drake too far and made the mistake of doing it in front of others. He was left with no choice, and now her back will forever carry the marks." Desiree closed her eyes and a tear slipped from the corner as Mica continued. "That's why she doesn't live with the nest. It took a lot from her to go back there with us and fight last night. She fought the other clan and risked facing Drake again for us. I know this goes against your independent nature, and I love that part of you. If it makes you feel better you can argue all you want with me in private. In fact, I look forward to it, but to cross Drake purposefully is dangerous for both of us. Do you understand?" She relaxed in his arms and nodded. "If I remove my hand, will you stop arguing?" She opened her eyes and nodded again. He kissed the top of her head and dropped his hand.

She turned in his arms, burying her face in his chest, sobbing. "My God, Denise, I had no idea. It must have been awful."

Her crying over Denise surprised him. Not two days ago she herself had thrown a fireball at Denise for her smart mouth. Denise hadn't liked the idea that he was involved with a human and had played a huge part in an elaborate plan to separate them. It had almost worked too. Desiree was devastated when Denise lied and claimed to be his mate. When he forced Denise to tell Desiree the truth, Denise had made the mistake of making light of the situation.

He reached out and touched her mind. *You're crying over Denise? I did not tell you about her to make you cry for her. I was just trying to warn you—to make a point.*

She sniffed. *I know, but Denise is my friend.*

Friend? Since when?

She and I connected in the cave. I like her. If it hadn't been for Caleb—

She wouldn't have been there causing trouble in the first place. He finished for her.

Yeah.

You have a very large heart and are very protective of those you love. Please, just let Sherry be. For whatever reason, Drake seems to be attracted to her. To cross him—

She wiped the tears from her eyes, then gazed into his, giving him a watery smile. *Back off. I get it.* He nodded. *I promise to try. I see that my punishment would not just hurt me. I love you, Mica. I couldn't bear to see you hurt because of something I did. I promise to let Sherry be, unless—*

Unless?

She shrugged. *If she comes running to me for help, I can't turn my back on her.*

Promise me that you will come to me before you do or say anything foolish.

I will try—in the heat of the moment, it doesn't seem foolish at the time.

Mica shook his head in exasperation and wrapped her in his arms. *It looks like my safest bet is to keep you as far away from Drake as I can.*

Good luck with that. I am his slave, remember?

Mica sighed. *How can I forget?*

***

Sherry watched the silent exchange between Desiree and Mica. She was happy that her friend had finally found love, she just hoped that Desiree wouldn't do something stupid like crossing Drake. She smiled when she saw Desiree smile up at Mica. "I'm happy for you kiddo," she whispered.

"You are beautiful when you smile."

Sherry hadn't realized that Drake had been watching her until he spoke. Her body betrayed her, reacting to his tone by flushing hot. She glanced up to see him smiling at her. Her heart just about stopped. He had to be one of the most handsome men she had ever seen.

"It sounds a bit like a pickup line to me."

Drake looked confused. "Pickup line?" She nodded. "Please explain."

She laughed lightly. "Explain what?"

He crossed his arms over his chest, studying her carefully. "I've never heard the term before. What is a pickup line?"

Her eyes rounded. "You're serious, you don't know?"

Drake shrugged. "I've not been out much in the last fifty years. Please explain."

"Well, um, a lot of guys lie and tell a girl untrue things, like she's beautiful, to get her to go out with them or sleep with them."

During her explanation, the smile dropped from Drake's face and was replaced with a scowl. "I do not lie."

Sherry took a step back. "I wasn't implying that you do—uh, just maybe stretched the truth a bit." He lifted an eyebrow and continued to glare. "Oh, come on Drake, I am not beautiful. You have eyes, you have to see the same thing I see when I look into the mirror. Maybe you've been cooped up in that warehouse too long. The attention you've shown me is flattering, but—"

"You think I am playing some sort of human game in order to trick you into my bed?"

She crossed her arms over her chest. "Well, aren't you?"

"I speak the truth; you are beautiful. I do not need to resort to human tricks. If I want you in my bed, you will be there. I will have no need of human games to get you there, either."

Her mouth dropped open. "If you think you're going to force me, then think again, bucko."

When he grinned, exposing his fangs, she took a hesitant step back. "I will not need to force you, love. You will beg me to take you."

He took a step toward her and she retreated another step. "Never."

"Never is a very long time."

The softness in his tone rolled over her, then through her. Her nipples beaded and heat settled at her core. "Stop that."

He caught her change in scent and chuckled. He knew exactly what he was doing to her. "I have not touched you, love."

She didn't think this was the least bit funny. Just the sound of his voice made her ache for him. He was right, she would be begging...she was almost to that point now. She had to get away, now, because if he touched her again she would be a goner.

She averted her eyes and stepped around him, figuring that maybe if she ignored him he would give up. She rubbed her hands briskly over her chilled arms. "Can we go now? This place is kinda creeping me out."

Desiree glanced at Drake, then at Mica, unsure how to respond. "Sure, kiddo, I guess." She looked to Drake and shrugged.

Drake flipped out his cell phone, bringing up the speed dial. "Sean, bring the Hummer to the mausoleums." He paused. "Yes, we have the women." He paused again. "I know the sun is up.... Idiot," he growled under his breath. "Go into my chamber and get three amulets, and bring two others with you." Drake looked at his phone, cursing under his breath. "Tell me again why I put up with you? Take one of the amulets for yourself, then give one to Jacob and the other to Jonah. They're my best trackers.... Because Justin Hargrove got away...you know what? Just send Jacob and

Jonah, give the other amulet to Tracy. You stay at the warehouse.... Because if I see you right now, I'll rip your fucking throat out." Mica laughed out loud and Drake glared back. "*We need the Hummer, now!*" he yelled into the phone.

Sherry started when he snapped the phone shut. Mica was still laughing, but she was leery about standing too close to an angry vampire. Skirting the smashed coffin, she sat down next to Desiree on the bench.

Mica stood and clapped his friend on the back. "Trouble in paradise?"

Drake bared his teeth when he growled, dropping his fangs. Still grinning, Mica took a step back.

"You're walking on thin ice," was Drake's reply.

***

Sherry sat in the back seat of the Hummer next to Drake. Another vampire, Tracy, one of Drake's trackers, was behind the wheel. They were headed toward her house.

"I don't know why you wouldn't let me ride home with Desiree and Mica," Sherry said again for the fifth time.

Drake refused to answer after the second time.

Sherry sighed heavily. "I need to go pick up my car."

"I'll have your car delivered. For now you're not leaving my sight."

"This is ridiculous."

"Hargrove is on the loose. Normally a mere human wouldn't cause me much concern. We'd track him down and eliminate the threat. However, if he's anything like his father, then he's a crafty little bastard. Desiree had to turn his father into a rat and cage him to stop him. I'll not leave you unprotected."

Sherry crossed her arms over her chest and huffed. "I don't see what this has to do with me. He wasn't after me. He was after Desiree. Go bug her."

"She has Mica to protect her. I'm concerned about you. You know he's a witch hunter, love. He knows you're a witch, and he'll be after you too."

She looked out the side glass. "Fine...whatever."

He laughed softly. "You *are* stubborn."

She turned her head and glared, taking exception to his laughter. "Get used to it. I'm just getting started. You'll want to be rid of me soon enough."

"Somehow I doubt that. I've been around for over three hundred years. After a while things get a little mundane. So far you've been quite entertaining. Not only are you beautiful, but you possess a fiery spirit. Being in your company will prove to be anything but boring."

Arrogant bastard, I'd love to wipe that cocky grin off his face, she thought as she rolled her eyes at his statement. "That's wonderful; I amuse you, glad to hear it." Her voice dripped with sarcasm. "Whatever do I do for an encore?"

His grin broadened as his eyes emanated an unnatural glow. "I can think of a few—" The scowl she gave him stopped him in mid-sentence. The car coming to a stop in front of her house allowed him the reprieve to change the subject. "We're here."

A smile touched her lips as she breathed a sigh of relief. "Great. I just want to go into the house, take a bubble bath, then go to bed and forget this day ever happened."

She grabbed the door handle and shot out of the car.

***

A bubble bath and bed, hummm, that sounds intriguing, he thought. He only paused a moment to appreciate the twitch in her hips as she rushed toward the front door. Her short skirt left little to the imagination.

His cock hardened in anticipation, the ache intensifying with each delicate step. He couldn't remember ever being this obsessed with a human before. All he could think about was burying himself deep within her and hearing her scream out his name as her body quaked and milked him with her own orgasm. His cock twitched and strained against the zipper with that thought. "I'll have you yet," he said under his breath.

"Sire?"

"Take the Hummer back to the warehouse. I'm staying here. I'll call when I'm ready for you to pick us up."

Tracy turned in the seat. "*Us*, sire?"

Drake spoke as he slid out of the SUV. "Yes, she'll be staying with us. It's no longer safe for her here."

Tracy grinned, exposing his fangs. "The witch is not going to like that one bit."

Drake leaned into the Hummer slightly before closing the door. "I'm counting on it." He heard Tracy's laughter as the door closed.

***

As soon as Desiree placed her purse on the end table Mica swept her off her feet and sat down on the couch with her in his lap. "I want to hear no more arguments about a body guard. Hargrove could have killed you and your friend today, and if we hadn't bonded it would have taken me a lot longer to find you. As it is you need healing, again." He smiled. "It seems that the last time I rescued you from a Hargrove your face was in the same condition." He raised an eyebrow. "Are they naturally abusive men or...."

She smiled sheepishly. "I guess I don't know when to shut up." She furrowed her brow. "What do you mean 'need healing again,' as if you had healed me? I healed on my own last time, thank you very much," she said in irritation, then his smile grew. "Are you implying that you could have healed me?"

71

"I—hmmm—I sense that to tell the truth will irritate you. However, you did heal immediately after we bonded."

Did I? she thought, searching her memories. Her eyes widened. *I did.* "How did you do that?"

"You drank from me when we bonded. My blood has healing properties."

"If you could have healed me all along, then why didn't you offer to heal me sooner?"

"At the time I didn't think you would be too cooperative with me opening a vein and telling you to drink. Also, there was the issue that I was supposed to deliver you to Drake and leave. Giving you my blood would have given us a connection. I would have always been able to feel you."

"Would that have been so bad?"

"To walk around with a perpetual hard on for a woman I couldn't have? What do you think?"

She laughed. "Um, knowing you, I believe that you probably would have killed someone or challenged Drake for me."

"I believe I did that last night." Mica said, and the smile fell from Desiree's face as she remembered the events. Drake had refused to let her leave with Mica, and they nearly fought. She had threatened to throw a fireball at Drake. They were very fortunate that he found humor in the situation. "Lucky for us that Drake didn't have us both put to death for treason."

Desiree shuddered. "Drake is dangerous. Mica, I'm worried about Sherry."

Mica sighed. "I don't think he'll harm her. I haven't seen Drake show this kind of an attraction to a woman since his wife died."

"I thought you said that when mates bond, if something happened to either of them the other would die." Mica nodded. "If that's the case, then why isn't Drake dead now?"

"I said wife, not mate. He was married to her when he was still human. She died in childbirth along with the babe."

"Women have babies every day; it's generally no big deal. What happened?"

"This was a little over three hundred years ago. Many women didn't survive childbirth back then. The child was breech, and she bled to death. Drake blamed himself." Mica frowned as he thought back. "Come to think of it, there are many things about Sherry that resemble Cara. Her hair color is about the same, and her eyes. Yes, her eyes resemble Cara's."

"Sherry is *not* Cara."

"I know, and I know Drake knows that too. It just might explain his sudden interest in your friend."

***

Is it even still the same day? Sherry wondered as she dug through her purse looking for her house keys. So much had changed in the course of a few hours. She was physically and emotionally exhausted. Her attempts at resisting Drake were wearing her out. Her mind was at constant war with her hormones, her body betraying her at every turn. *Just concentrate on getting inside,* she thought. *He'll grow bored waiting in the car and will eventually give up. Desiree's right. I got a little too close to the flame and I'm gonna get burned if I'm not careful. Where are those keys, dammit?* She pushed her wallet aside and her fingers grazed the key ring. *Yes.*

As she pulled the keys free, Drake plucked them from her fingers.

She frowned, reaching for the keys. "Hey, what do you think you're doing? I thought you were still in the car."

He jingled them just out of her reach, flashing a smile. "I'm opening the door. I can't protect you from the car."

As if to reinforce his words, the Hummer pulled away from the curb and rounded the corner, disappearing from sight. She was now alone with Drake, and that scared the hell out of her. With as much resolve as she could muster she looked him squarely in the eyes. "I'm not inviting you inside. Vampires can't come into a person's home unless they're invited." At least she hoped they couldn't.

He turned the key in the lock, pushed open the door, and crossed the threshold. "That's a myth, love." He continued down the hall, checking every corner.

She stomped her foot in frustration, then chased after him. "Stop, Drake, I didn't invite you into my home. Where do you think you're going?" She ran up behind him. "You are not king in my home. This is my castle, not yours." She reached out, grabbing his arm to stop him. She knew what she said was childish, but there was no way she wanted him traipsing about her home like he owned it.

He paused briefly, chucking her under the chin. "I am king everywhere, and as such I do not need your permission." Her mouth dropped open in disbelief. "And as to where I am going, I'm making sure the place is secure." He turned and continued toward her bedroom.

She stood rooted to her spot, dumbfounded. She watched him walk right into her bedroom like he owned the place. Her mind raced frantically. *What am I gonna do? He's gotta go, but how?* She managed to get her feet to move then stood in her doorway, watching him investigate everything. *Think, think, think....* She turned her head and spotted her jewelry box. She smiled triumphantly as she marched toward her dresser.

Drake caught her movement and stopped to watch her. She knew he was still watching her as she turned her back to him. She could feel it like a physical caress. Grabbing the box, she rummaged through the jewelry, laughing softly to herself. Her fingers plucked the gold cross and chain from the clutter. *Yes, this should do it.* Placing the chain around her neck she turned around and thrust her chest forward, smiling broadly. "See how well you handle this, sire."

Karen Fuller

Chapter Ten

"Hmmm, an offer." His voice was low and sexy. Her eyes rounded, and his smile broadened at her reaction. He ran his finger over the cross, then let his fingers drop to caress her breast. Her nipples pebbled. "Not quite begging, but—"

"Oh, shit...." She tried to take a step back but was already wedged against the dresser, so she placed her palms against his chest to push him away. She had thought she was clever putting on the cross, but the instant she had uttered the words she saw her mistake. "I, uh, that's not what I meant."

"Your lovely lips speak words of denial...." Pulling her to him he brushed his lips lightly over hers. Her arms relaxed and her body melted into his. He cupped her butt cheeks and pulled her up against his hard erection. "But your body betrays you. It knows what you want...." Placing feather soft kisses down her neck, he hovered over the vein pulsing at the base. Her pulse quickened beneath his tongue as he ran it over the sweet spot, drawing it into his mouth but not biting. "What you need...." He slid his hand beneath her skirt; his fingers inched beneath the elastic of her panties to caress her butt. "What you crave."

Sherry couldn't think. Her body was in a fervor. The fiery caresses and soft-spoken words ignited a sudden craving to be his. Need churned in the pit of her belly, settling in her core, cream soaking her panties. These new sensations took over and pushed the voice in her head screaming *dangerous* into the background.

He knew the instant she let down her guard and slipped his finger between her soft folds, pumping in and out of her. She rocked her hips, soaking his hand with her juices. "Oh, God," she moaned. "What's happening to me?"

"You are discovering what it means to be a woman, love." He added a finger, stretching her, plunging deeper as her inner walls pulsated. "You are so tight."

She writhed over his fingers, her breath coming out in short pants. "I've never—"

"Let yourself go, love. Just feel."

Just feel? She didn't know what to feel. Every nerve ending in her body was hypersensitive. The sensations were building to an almost unbearable level, but she didn't want it to stop, not ever. "Please...I need...."

He laughed softly, withdrew his fingers, then took a small step back.

Sherry's eyes flew open in confusion and sexual frustration, her body aching for his touch. "Why did you stop? I thought...." She shook her head and wrapped her arms around herself self-consciously. "You're laughing at me—why?"

"I just wanted to prove a point."

A point? Her breathing was slowly coming under her control again as her body cooled a bit, allowing her to think. "Obviously I miss your point, because I don't understand."

"My point was that I told you that you would beg me to."

And I begged, ran through her head. Sudden anger and embarrassment washed over her. "*Why you arrogant son-of-a-bitch!*" In a flash, her hand snaked up to slap the smug look from his face, but his reflexes were faster, catching her wrist in midair. She tried to yank her hand back as she yelled, *"Let me go!"*

"No, we're going to finish this."

"The hell we will." She balled up her fist on the other hand and took a swing and him. He dodged that blow too and pinned both hands over her head. She squealed in frustration, then narrowed her eyes, panting with her struggles. "Just wait until I get loose."

His smile broadened. "A little hellcat—mmm, I love your spirit. You'll make an excellent warrior—and lover."

"Lover!" she spat. "Fuck you! I wouldn't sleep with you now if you were the last man on earth."

Undaunted, he pulled her sweater up over her head and past her hands before she even realized he had loosened his grip. He cupped her breast, running his thumb across her nipple peeking through the lace, then rolled the marbled bud between his fingers. "The thought of sleeping hadn't crossed my mind."

She stomped her foot and tried to pull her hands free. "Stop that."

He smirked, ignoring her command as his nimble fingers popped the front clasp, and her heavy breasts swung free of the lacy fabric. His eyes now focused on her exposed skin, and against her will the rosy peaks puckered under his gaze. "You're so beautiful. I've desired to taste you from the moment I laid eyes on you." He pulled her to him, pressing her body against his hard erection. Then he nuzzled her neck, inhaling her scent. "Ambrosia—your scent is intoxicating. It's an alluring mixture of your arousal and...." He rubbed his cheek against hers, inhaling again. "And—innocence...a virgin."

Her heart hammered in her chest. *He knows.* She renewed her struggles, now suddenly afraid. She didn't fear the loss of her innocence, it was the fear of losing herself. Her body was no longer her own. It now craved *his* touch. She wanted more and hated herself for it.

"Please…don't," she said, but her resolve sounded weak even to her own ears. Unable to move, she watched with morbid fascination as he knelt down, lowered his head, and drew the aching peak between his lips and suckled. She threw back her head and licked her lips as sharp waves of pleasure spread throughout her body, leaving her writhing beneath his skilled mouth.

Sherry was so wrapped up in feeling that she didn't notice when he had let go of her arms. She was now holding on to the back of his head, cupping her breast with the other hand and feeding it to him. She felt him run his hands down her hips and smoothly slide her skirt and panties down her legs. She shivered as his lips now traveled across her abs, and the sharp pangs of need throbbed to new heights. Entwining her fingers in his hair, she moaned. "Please…don't…stop."

He looked up into her eyes, staring intensely. His were dark and smoldering, then he grinned and stood.

Her mouth dropped open. *No not again*, then she panicked. She frowned, shaking her head frantically. "Don't you *dare* stop."

He chuckled, sweeping her off her feet and crushing her against his chest as he walked toward the bed. "No matter how tempting it is to pin that luscious body of yours up against that wall, bury my cock deep within your liquid heat, and have my fill, I'm not that selfish."

Sherry's frown intensified as she squirmed in his arms to get away. "Put me down and stop toying with me."

He kissed the tip of her nose and tightened his grip. "I'm not toying with you."

"Drake, so help me...." She huffed out a long breath of exasperation. "Just put me down so that I can go take a cold shower and get dressed." She looked away to avoid his eyes and lowered her voice. "I think I've suffered enough humiliation for one day. I'd like to forget about you and this day ever happening."

"Love, look at me."

She refused to look at him. "Just let me go...please."

She squealed in surprise as he tossed her onto the bed. He untucked his shirt then pulled it up over his head. Sherry's eyes rounded as he exposed his massive muscular chest and rock hard abs. Her gaze dropped to the bulge straining his leather pants.

***

He had never dealt with a reluctant woman before, one that turned hot and cold within a second. When he tossed her on the bed he had every intention of ravaging her, by force if necessary. He was tired of the games. But he saw her eyes darken and her nipples pebble as she stared at his crotch; there was something erotic about that, so he decided to take another tactic and purposefully slowed his movements. After toeing off his boots, he slipped his pants half way down his hips, freeing his cock and fisting it with slow deliberate stokes.

***

She sat up and licked her lips, her eyes focused on his every movement. Her heart hammered in her chest. *My God,* she thought, *he's perfect. This can't be real; I must be dreaming or still back in that coffin in the mausoleum having dark fantasies.* She reached out her hand to touch, but thought better of it and pulled it back. But his hand grabbed hers and guided her fingers to the hot silky flesh.

He placed his hand over hers—guiding her movements—showing her how to please him. He was relieved when he let go to remove his pants that she kept up on her own, growing bolder as he lengthened and grew harder in her hands. He clenched his teeth together as his cock twitched, pre-cum seeping from the engorged head. "I won't last long if you keep that up, love." He placed both hands over hers to stop her movements. "When I come I want to be buried deep in your tight sheath with it pulsating around my cock, milking me in the throes of your own pleasure. But…." She shivered, then raised her gaze to his. "I want to pleasure you first." She bit her bottom lip. "I want to hear you scream out my name when you come for the first time, and I'll make sure you come many times before I'll even consider letting you out of this bed."

She just nodded, afraid to say anything in fear that this fantasy would shatter. She was thoroughly convinced that her mind was indeed fabricating this. Things like this just didn't happen to her.

Chapter Eleven

Drake knelt on the bed over her and covered her mouth with his. He slipped his tongue between her parted lips as he eased her down onto the mattress and he lay down beside her. His tongue stroked hers as his hands caressed and explored her body.

Her legs parted as his hand slipped between them. She was wet and ached for his touch.

She whimpered when he broke the kiss and rose above her. He briefly watched her expression change to wonder, then lust, as he plunged his fingers deep within her, pumping and stretching as she writhed on the bed, clutching the sheets in her fists.

He continued the tender assault with his mouth as he traveled down her body, tasting and suckling as her flesh twitched beneath his lips. Then he settled himself between her legs and draped her calves over his shoulders.

Her eyes flew open in surprise and she struggled a bit. "Drake?"

He grabbed her hips firmly, staying her movements. "Relax, love. I intend to teach you the pleasures of the flesh. You will enjoy yourself more if you let it happen. Just trust me."

She took a quivering breath, then expelled it slowly. He had her body wound tight and she needed release. "Okay." Her gaze met his. "I trust you."

"Good. Then close those beautiful eyes and let me have my wicked way with you." His tone was teasing.

She smiled as she closed her eyes, responding to his teasing tone. "Yes, sire."

"Prepare yourself, vixen; to tease and tempt a king comes with dire consequences." Her eyes flew open again. "You will get no rest tonight."

She laughed softly, warming up to the playful side of his personality that she hadn't seen until now. "I am nothing but your humble servant, sire. I place my body in your care."

He lifted an eyebrow and smacked her on the ass, then massaged the abused area. "You shall be no one's servant, vixen. You will be my queen."

She blinked at him in surprise.

He plunged three fingers deep within her, pumping in and out as he rubbed his thumb over her swollen nub. She caught her breath, raising her hips to the rhythm of his fingers as her eyes rolled beneath shuttered lids.

"Say it," he breathed. "Say the words."

She whimpered, her head thrashing from side to side. The sensations running through her body were intoxicating. She couldn't think.

"Say the words little one, and I will bring you sweet release." His fingers continued the assault, keeping her throbbing around them, hovering on the brink with no release.

"I will be your queen," she panted. "I'll be anything you want me to be…just please…."

He lifted her hips with his free hand, bringing her up to his mouth, then ran his tongue over the swollen nub. She cried out as her juices soaked his fingers. He covered her with his mouth and his tongue replaced his fingers, plunging into her creamy depths. Her inner walls gripped his tongue, soaking him as she shouted out his name and came hard.

***

He kissed her inner thigh while she was still coming down and rubbed his tongue over the sensitive area, releasing his venom to numb it. He wrapped his hand around his cock, stroking it as his fangs sank into her tender flesh, releasing the endorphins from his venom into her bloodstream, marking her as his. He then drank the virginal blood from her femoral artery, sealing the bond with her soul. This was a very intimate act for a vampire, bringing its own highs. He withdrew his fangs and sealed the tiny wounds. His cock ached…it was now time to seal the bond with her body.

He lowered her hips to where her legs now draped across his thighs. He reached up to tweak her nipples to wake her. They puckered beneath his fingers.

She caught her breath and opened her eyes.

He smiled. "I told you that there would be no rest for you tonight."

She placed her hand over her face, then peeked at him from between her fingers. "I can't believe I fell asleep."

He stroked his cock. "Your desires were sated temporarily, but you left me awake to entertain myself."

She giggled.

"Vixon, you should know better than to giggle at a man."

"Sorry." She reached out, taking the silky member into her hands, running her thumb over the engorged head. He sucked in a breath. "Will it always be like that…? The sex, I mean."

He shook his head. "No."

Her expression fell, and he could see her disappointment.

"No, little one, it will only get better."

85

Her eyes rounded. "I don't know if my heart can take it. I thought it would burst before and I'd die from the sensation."

He smiled at her innocent remark and ran his hands down her body, then stroked his fingers between her legs. "You'll live to love it, vixen. I'll show you what it's like to have your sweet body worshiped by a vampire." He leaned forward and grazed his lips across her neck, and felt the responding goose bumps travel beneath his lips. "Wrap your arms around my neck and hold on."

She wrapped her arms around his neck and he lifted her from the mattress, his palms supporting her butt. "Now wrap your legs around my waist. That's right." He lowered her to just above his throbbing member. "The first time will hurt you a little, but it won't last. I'll try to take it slow."

She nodded. "I still trust you."

He slanted his mouth over hers and plunged his tongue inside, stroking her tongue with his. She kissed him back with abandon as he eased her down over his cock. He pumped his hips, feeling her wet sheath stretch to accommodate his size. He slowly rocked his hips, plunging deeper. He felt her tense when he reached her barrier. Knowing there was no other way around it, he pushed through it, seating himself to the hilt. She whimpered and he froze to allow her time to adjust to his size. It was all he could do not to move. She was so tight and hot, it was a sweet torture. She rocked her hips, and then again, her juices coated him. He couldn't wait any longer and he began to thrust in and out of her. He grazed his lips over her throat while she threw her head back in abandon. He couldn't believe how passionate she was as she matched him stroke for stroke. It had been a long time, years in fact, since he had even cared about a woman's body beneath him, other than to slack his lust. He would enjoy spending time with this one. He felt justified in marking her. After all, she had agreed to be his queen. Her breathing picked up and her breasts bounced with the increased rhythm of their bodies locked as one. He felt her hot walls spasm around his cock, milking him, and he let himself go. He thrust harder and felt the roar start at his cock and expel from his lungs. He bit down on her sweet spot as the cum spilled from his body, filling her.

***

She shuddered again as he laid down on his back with her straddled on top of him; he was still buried deep within her. Her breathing was slowly coming back under her control. "My God," she panted softly. "I'm still tingling all over." She propped up on her elbows, resting her chin in her hands. As she gazed into his eyes she said, "Can I keep you?" He raised an eyebrow at her question, causing her to laugh. "Chill, sire, I was only teasing you."

With a growl he flipped her over onto her back and plunged deeper into her. "What if I won't let you go?"

Her heart raced. *He can't be serious, can he?*

He started to move again and she didn't give it another thought.

Chapter Twelve

The morning rays peeked through the blinds, shining into Sherry's eyes. As she stretched she felt Drake's grip tighten around her, and the memories of the night before washed over her. He had indeed kept her up most of the night and she felt a bit sore, but just thinking about the things he had done to her and with her made her wet all over again. Her stomach grumbled, then she heard Shadow's soft meow coming from the kitchen, so she eased out from beneath Drake's arm and headed to the kitchen.

As Sherry put on a pot of coffee and fed the cat, her thoughts drifted to the events of the day before. She had to admit that this morning was certainly different from any other. Drake was first and foremost on her mind. He was certainly the most gorgeous man she had ever seen, definitely arrogant and a bit overbearing, but there was something about him…. She caught herself grinning for no reason at all, then laughed out loud, causing Shadow to stop eating and stare. He tilted his head, then trotted out of the room. "Strange cat," she said to the empty room.

Her stomach rumbled again, and she realized that she hadn't eaten a thing since breakfast at the diner yesterday. She was suddenly starving. Opening the refrigerator, she stared at the contents. Deciding on bacon and eggs, she placed them on the counter, then paused. *Do vampires eat? Just call Desiree and ask her,* she reasoned.

She picked up her cell phone from the counter and noticed that she had three missed calls, all from Desiree. *Three calls?* Sherry frowned at the phone. *I wonder what was so urgent.* "Hmmm."

Her finger pressed redial and Desiree answered on the first ring. "Sherry, are you okay?" Desiree nearly shouted into the phone.

Desiree's panic irked her. "I'm *fine,* Mom! Why wouldn't I be?"

"It's just that you were *alone* with Drake all night."

Sherry sighed. "Des, in case you haven't noticed recently, I'm twenty-three now, not thirteen."

"I know, I know, but I know how overbearing and forceful Drake can be. I'm just worried, that's all. I was afraid that he'd force you—"

"He didn't *force* me to do anything." Sherry smiled to herself. "Let's just say that we worked it all out. He's amazing."

"Your meaning?"

"I don't kiss and tell."

"You had sex with him, didn't you? *Didn't you?*" Sherry pulled the phone away from her ear as Desiree shouted into the receiver. Sherry heard Mica in the background telling Desiree to calm down.

Sherry was angry now. Desiree was taking the protection issue a bit too far. "Yes, *Mom,* I did. I never knew that my sex life, or lack thereof, was any of your business. But it doesn't seem like you are going to let the subject drop without an answer, so here it is…it was amazing, mind-blowing in fact. It was the best damn night of my life. Happy now?"

"Did he mark you?" she shouted.

90

Mark me? What in the hell is she talking about? "What?"
"Did he claim you?"

Sherry rolled her eyes. "He claimed my virginity, nosy." She heard Desiree's sharp intake of breath and calmed down. "I haven't a clue as to what else you could be talking about, claiming."

"Sherry, I'm so sorry. I feel like this is all my fault."

"Look, Desiree, there's no need to be sorry. He can be an ass, yes, but I really like him. I've never felt this drawn to someone before. I don't have much experience in this kind of situation, but I think he really likes me too. But with guys, who knows?"

"I think he more than *likes* you."

"Good, I hope you're right." She heard Desiree sigh on the other end. "Des, you know what it's like to be a witch. The locals shunning you in fear of what you might do to them; the feeling when a new guy comes into town and he seems to like you, and you think to yourself, 'now finally'; then the next thing you know someone's whispering in his ear and you never see him again. Drake is not afraid of me. He's a little intimidating, but I actually discovered a playful side to him last night, and it really surprised me."

"Playful? Drake?"

Sherry giggled. "Yeah, I was teasing him, calling him sire. He teased me back and called me his queen. He actually made me *say* that I was his queen or he wouldn't...never mind. That's too much information. But I'll admit that that game was...interesting, to say the least."

"Hang on a second, Sherry." Sherry heard muffled talking in the background, then Desiree came back on the phone. "Sherry, just please be careful. Drake is dangerous. Mica says that Drake doesn't play games."

"You just tell Mica that he's wrong about Drake. He's not as tough as he appears. He's actually quite caring."

Desiree sighed. "I hope you're right."

"I am right. Stop worrying. Um, Desiree I actually called for another reason."

"Oh?"

"Yeah, Drake's still sleeping and I'm starving. I was going to cook breakfast for us but I don't even know if vampires eat."

"I had the same question with Mica. They *can* eat food, but generally don't. It doesn't satisfy their hunger and they don't crave food anymore."

"Thanks for the info. We'll probably see you both later. I'm gonna eat something before I fall over. Later."

"Bye, Sherry."

***

Thoroughly sated, Drake hadn't slept that well in years. He opened his eyes and was startled to find himself nose to nose with a black ball of fur. "Where in the hell did you come from?"

Shadow sat down on Drake's chest, his intelligent green eyes seeming to mock him as he placed his paw on Drake's chin. Drake frowned as Shadow began to purr, circled his chest, then curled up in a ball and laid his head down.

Sherry walked into the bedroom. She wore a long white terrycloth robe, and had her hands wrapped around a steaming cup of coffee. She paused next to the bed and stared at the cat. "Hmmmm—interesting." She smiled at Drake as she reached over and stroked her pet. "He seems to like you—which is odd. He doesn't usually trust strangers, especially men."

Drake picked the cat up, holding him in front of him, and stared into his eyes. He sat up and looked at Sherry, frowning. "How long have you owned this fur ball?"

She huffed out an exasperated breath. "Drake, that's not very nice. Shadow is—"

"How long?"

She shrugged. "I don't know—two years, maybe. He showed up on my doorstep right after I moved in. He's my familiar. Why?"

He put Shadow down on the bed, then crossed his arms over his chest. "Your *pet* isn't what he seems."

Sherry smirked. "What, you can talk to animals? He told you that he has some deep dark desire to harm me or something?" She brought the coffee cup up to her lips.

"If that were the case then he would be dead right now. No, I can't talk to animals, but I can recognize shape shifters." Shadow hung his head and looked toward the door.

Sherry's eyes bugged as she choked on her coffee. "*Shape shifter!*" She coughed a few more times as Shadow backed slowly toward the edge of the bed, away from Sherry's reach. "*Shadow!* The whole time...." Her eyes bugged again and she slammed her coffee cup down on the dresser. "*The whole time?*" Shadow froze, trembling. "All that time I *knew* you understood me, but I thought the reason was because you were my familiar and I thought we had a connection. But you understood me because you're not even a cat. You watched me change and take baths...you little pervert!"

Drake laughed softly. "Calm down, Vixen."

She pointed toward Shadow. "I find a traitor in my home and you find this funny?"

"He is just a child."

"What?"

93

"He is just a child," he repeated. "If he were here to harm you he would have done it a long time ago. My guess is he is hiding from something or someone, and you were safe." Drake nodded toward the cat. "Reveal yourself."

The air around the cat shimmered and formed into a boy of about twelve. His black wavy hair was long and in bad need of a trim. He was a handsome kid with large green eyes. He looked away, clearly ashamed of his nudity.

Sherry opened her top drawer and tossed him a t-shirt. "Here, put this on."

He slipped it over his head and mumbled, "Thank you."

Sherry sat down on the bed next to Drake, studying the boy carefully. "Wait, I know you." He nodded. "Oh my god, you're Mica...you've grown so much, I didn't recognize you. Honey, we thought you were dead." She brought her hand up to cover her sob as her eyes filled with tears. "Your poor mother. I'm so sorry. We thought you had burned in the fire too. If we had known...."

His bottom lip quivered. "I should have died with her."

Sherry rose from the bed and walked to the other side, taking the child into her arms, hugging him to her. "Don't ever say that." She took a step back and took a good look at him. "Why didn't you come to me? I would've opened my home to you."

He winced. "Aunt Sher, I did."

She cut her eyes at him, shaking her head. "I meant as a human boy. Your mother never told me that your father was a shifter. I had no idea that this was even possible."

Drake looked between the two. "Mica? That's not a real common name."

The boy shrugged. "My mom said that I was named after my father's best friend."

Drake's frown deepened. "Sherry, how did you know his mother?"

"Celia was in our coven, and she was one of my best friends."

"Did you know Mica's father?"

Sherry shook her head. "Celia was very secretive about him. Then they had a fight or something and she never saw him again. A few weeks later she found out she was pregnant with Mica. We begged her to tell him about the child, but she refused. She said it wasn't safe, whatever that meant."

Drake smiled for the first time since discovering the boy. "The pieces are starting to come together."

Sherry tilted her head. "I don't understand."

Drake gestured to the boy. "You know the boy's father's best friend."

"No, I don't...I...." Her eyes widened. "Desiree's mate, Mica?"

Drake nodded. "Mica's best friend is—"

"Caleb." Sherry interjected. At the mention of Caleb's name the boy's eyes grew fearful as he backed away toward the door. Sherry grabbed his arm. "You know the name."

Mica tugged at her grip. "Please, Aunt Sher, lemme go. I don't want you to die too, like my mom did."

Her grip tightened. "The fire wasn't an accident?"

The tears streamed down his face as he shook his head and tugged harder to get away. "When the men came they were pounding on the door, shouting for Caleb to come out or else. My mom was so scared, Aunt Sher, and I was too. She told me to run and hide. I ran into the kitchen and shifted into a cat for the first time. I didn't even know I could do that. I hid behind the couch and I saw everything."

Sherry sat down in the chair and pulled him into her lap. "Tell me."

"Mom shouted at the door and told those men that she hadn't seen or talked to Caleb in ten years and that they needed to leave. They didn't believe her. They busted down the front door and four of them came into the living room. They were big men like him." Mica pointed toward Drake. "They told her that they came for the whelp. She shouted, 'You can't have him!' Then their leader shouted something about defying the alpha, and when he did they all changed into giant black cats. I watched the leader strike my mom down with his claws." His shoulders shook with grief. "Aunt Sher, Mom's eyes were open and she was covered in so much blood...she didn't move. I knew she was dead. I was little, but I had seen enough movies to know what a dead body looked like. I wanted to run to her, but I was scared. Then the leader ordered the other three to search the house and find the whelp. I didn't know what a whelp was, but if they killed Mom for it I wasn't sticking around to find out what it was, so I snuck out an open window and ran. When I looked back over my shoulder I saw the fire. I knew Mom was already dead so I kept running, and I didn't stop until I came here. I had nowhere else to go."

Drake reached over, picked his pants up off the floor, and fished the cell phone out of the pocket. He flipped it open and pressed the speed dial. "Mica."

The sound of Drake's voice drew Sherry's and the boy's attention.

"Where's Caleb?... Call him and have him meet us at the warehouse...There's someone he needs to meet." Drake listened quietly to what Mica was saying. "Yes, bring Desiree...this may concern her too." There was another pause, and Sherry could tell that Drake's patience was wearing thin. "Because it's time your friend learned that there are consequences for his actions.... No, this doesn't have anything to do with Hargrove or what happened in Tennessee. It has something to do with his pack.... I know, I know." Drake looked at Sherry and young Mica. "Be there in an hour."

Sherry squeezed Mica's shoulders and felt him tremble at the prospect of meeting his father. "Drake, what did you tell Mica that you know?"

"I'm not a hundred percent sure I know what happened between Caleb and his pack in England. I know he did something to cause them to turn on him, and I do remember Mica rescuing Caleb from the pack's alpha three hundred years ago. Caleb nearly died from his wounds and refused to talk to me about what happened. I know that Mica knows what happened, but he didn't talk about it either. The vampire wars had just ended and Caleb needed a fresh start, so all three of us set sail for America."

Mica nodded sadly, then he looked up. "Aunt Sher, do you know what a whelp is, and why they killed Mama for it?"

Sherry exchanged a nervous glance with Drake and he nodded. "A whelp is a cub or a baby. They were after Caleb's child."

"Me?" His eyes filled with fresh tears. "Mama died protecting me."

Sherry hugged him tight and let him cry. "Honey, it wasn't your fault. There was nothing you could do to prevent it. She loved you very much and wanted to protect you."

Karen Fuller

Chapter Thirteen

Sherry gave Mica a pair of sweat pants to go with the t-shirt, along with a pair of wool socks. She frowned. "Drake, he can't go out in public like that. It's the middle of February and he doesn't even have a pair of shoes, much less a jacket. It's cold outside."

Mica shrugged. "Aunt Sher, I can just phase back into a cat."

"No, you just spent the last two years as a cat. You need to acclimate yourself back to human life. You know, hold intelligent conversations, eat human food, stuff like that."

He wrinkled his nose. "I am a bit sick of *Fancy Feast*."

Sherry bit her lip to keep from laughing. "I bet you are." She ruffled his hair then sobered her expression. "You are *not* changing back into a cat, at least not today."

"Yes, ma'am."

Drake reached for his pants again. "I'll call Sean and have him get the boy some clothes, shoes and a jacket. I told Mica to meet us at the warehouse in an hour, so we need to get ready."

Sherry nodded. "Mica, go into the kitchen and fix yourself a bowl of cereal."

"But I've already eaten this morning, Aunt Sher."

She turned his shoulders toward the door. "Don't argue with me. Go get yourself a bowl of cereal and give us a few private moments to get dressed."

He smiled excitedly. "Can I have any kind I want?"

She smiled at his enthusiasm and ruffled his hair again. "Help yourself to whatever's in there."

"Thanks," he said as he took off toward the kitchen.

Sherry shut the bedroom door, then felt Drake's arms around her from behind. His hands slipped beneath her robe to cup her breasts. She closed her eyes and leaned into him as his lips nibbled on the curve of her neck, sending gooseflesh down her arms. She groaned as the now familiar throbbing settled between her legs. "Mmmm," she moaned. "We don't have...." He ran his hand down her body and slipped his fingers between her legs, halting her speech as he plunged two fingers into her wetness. As she rode his fingers she felt his erection press into her. She took a ragged breath, her body pulsating for release. "No time," she panted.

He growled into her ear, then nipped at her neck. "We will make the time, vixen. I haven't had my fill of you yet." She whimpered as he withdrew his fingers, then turned her toward the bed. Slipping the robe from her shoulders he said, "Bend over the bed and place your weight on your hands. I'm going to take you from behind."

Sherry felt his hands grip her hips as she bent over, and the engorged head probed her slick opening. She reached between her legs and wrapped her fingers around his hot flesh, guiding him in and squeezing as she ran her hand up and down the length of him. A smile touched her lips at his approving growl. "I could get used to this."

"So could I," he said as he rocked his hips forward.

She felt the size of him stretch and fill her as he slid in to the hilt. She swallowed hard, shuddering at the sensation. He only paused for a moment before he thrust his hips, pulling out only to enter again and again. She brought her hips back to meet his, with each stroke fully penetrating, fueling the need until it consumed them both. The climax took her by surprise as her entire body quaked with the sensation, her core pulsating around him. He pulled her hips back one last time, forcefully, bringing her upper body up against him. He ran his tongue over the vein at the crook of her neck, and she felt his fangs pierce her skin, but strangely there was no pain associated with it, only an intense feeling of euphoria. She came again with him as she felt him feed and his hot cum fill her.

***

The heavy wooden doors opened on their approach. The two guards at the door bowed as Drake and Sherry crossed the threshold. Sherry pulled Mica closer to her as she looked around. The place was full of vampires, and most compared in size to Drake. Sherry noticed that the majority of them refused to make eye contact and bowed their heads. "Stay close to me. I don't want you to wander off in here, it might not be safe."

Mica's eyes saucered as he gawked at the huge men. "Uh huh," he said weakly. "Not much chance of that."

"You are both safe here," Drake said. "No one would dare harm you."

Sherry took a deep breath then nodded. "Let's get this over with." She looked around the room. The large open area was tastefully decorated in bright Marti Gras colors. The room contained many chairs and couches. The furniture was deep brown leather, the pieces large and apparently specially made to accommodate the warriors. The colorful carpet stretched the length of the room, its main pattern the fleur-de-lis. Matching pillows were scattered about the room. The photos and paintings on the walls were of New Orleans in different stages in history. "Looks are deceiving. I would have never guessed this place existed from outside. It rivals Mica's mansion."

Drake smiled. "It's nice to hear the approval in your voice. We've made a great many improvements since Hurricane Katrina. As with everyone in New Orleans, we lost a lot when it flooded."

"Desiree was so adamant about not wanting to come here, I thought it must be like a dungeon or something…you know, dark and dank. It's actually quite nice. It's very…colorful, for lack of a better word."

"I find it comfortable. Ah, there's Sean." Drake motioned for Sean to approach. "Sean is one of my bodyguards."

Sherry studied Sean as he approached. As with all the vampires she had noticed since coming in, he was gorgeous, tall, blonde, and built, but not nearly the size of Drake or Mica. "Bodyguard?"

"Gopher, lackey, errand-boy…." He chuckled.

Sherry hid her smile behind her hand as Sean approached.

Sean bowed to Drake. "Sire, Mica, Desiree, and Caleb are waiting for you in the library. I would add that Caleb is a bit nervous. I believe he thinks that he is in trouble or something." Drake nodded. Sean studied the boy. "I have also laid out an assortment of clothes in the library for the boy. I'm sure something in there will fit him." Sean looked to Sherry. His eyes widened a bit with a look of surprise, then he bowed. When he rose he looked back to Drake. "The new queen has a son?"

"I can speak for myself," she huffed. She now had both their attention. "Why does everyone deem it necessary to talk around me like I'm not even in the room?"

102

Sean bowed again, then spoke to Drake. "I meant no disrespect, sire. I haven't been granted permission to speak to her directly yet."

This is ridiculous, he did it again, she thought. *The man is a buffoon, he called me a queen. If I were a queen I'd order his ass kicked for insolence.* She saw Drake smile. *No, it can't be. He couldn't have just heard my thoughts.*

"No, the boy is not hers."

You stubborn ass, you talked around me again.

Drake tilted his head and looked into her eyes. *Stubborn ass?*

Sherry's eyes rounded. *You* can *hear me.*

Yes.

How?

"Thank you, Sean. We'll all be in the library, and don't wish to be disturbed."

Sean bowed again. "Yes, sire." He left them.

Oh, no you don't, mister. You are not going to ignore me. I want some answers.

Later, vixen, we have others waiting.

Fine, but this isn't finished. She squeezed Mica's shoulders. "Let's go, hun."

"I'm afraid, Aunt Sher. What if...?"

"It'll be okay, hun, you'll see. Everything will work itself out. Keep your chin up and remember that you'll always have me. No matter what happens in there, I'll always be here for you, kiddo. I promise."

He nodded. "Okay."

Two guards stood on either side of the library doors and opened them when they approached. As they entered the library, Sherry saw Mica and Desiree exchange a startled glance, then Mica bowed low. "My queen."

Okay, this is beyond weird. Drake?

In a moment, love.

"What's this all about?" Caleb demanded in a defensive tone. "Who's the woman and the kid?"

Drake cocked an eyebrow at his tone. "Caleb, this is your son, Mica."

Caleb shook his head. "Oh, no you don't. You're not saddling a kid on me. I've never seen that woman before in my life. If she's claiming that—"

"*Enough!*" Drake roared. "You will be silent."

Caleb clamped his mouth shut and glared at Sherry.

"You see, Aunt Sher? I knew he wouldn't want me." The dejected tone in Mica's voice broke Sherry's heart.

She approached Caleb and slapped him hard across the face. "Why, you arrogant ass!"

Caleb's eyes turned, glowing amber, as he shook with anger.

Drake snatched Sherry away, out of Caleb's reach. His eyes glowed red, his voice cold and threatening. "Shift and it will be your final time."

Mica gripped Caleb's shoulders and shook his friend. "Caleb, don't!"

Desiree looked between Caleb and the boy. She smiled at the boy. "You're Celia's boy, aren't you?"

"Yes, ma'am."

"We all thought you were dead."

Caleb froze. "Celia. I haven't seen her in years."

Sherry crossed her arms over her chest. "Obviously."

"If she's claiming I'm the boy's father, then—"

Desiree frowned as she turned on Caleb. "Celia's dead, Caleb."

The look that crossed his face was first shock then sorrow. "I had no idea."

"It doesn't take a genius to see the resemblance between you two. Celia never told us who his father was."

"Those men killed her 'cause of you!" the boy yelled.

"What men?"

Drake crossed his arms over his chest. "From what the boy has told us, it sounds like it was your old pack from England. It appears that they were here to take your son. Celia died protecting the boy from a vengeance directed at you."

Caleb sat down hard. "I have a son," he said in disbelief. "She should have told me."

"A son *you* now need to protect from *your* pack," Drake said.

Caleb shook his head. "If he's mine, I'll protect him with my life, but with Celia gone how will I know for sure?"

Sherry frowned. "He's yours, trust me."

Caleb stared at Sherry hard. "I don't know you from Adam, lady."

"Caleb!" Mica interjected. "Watch your tone, she is Drake's queen."

Sherry caught her breath and looked sharply at Drake. *I'm your what?*

Queen. Her eyes bugged, then he continued out loud. "Mica, boy, show your father what you can do."

"Aunt Sher?" Sherry threw Drake an exasperated look, then nodded to the boy.

"Go ahead, honey. Show him."

The air shimmered around the boy as he shrunk down into the clothes. He poked his head from the opening of the sweatshirt.

"Shadow," Desiree said in surprise. She turned to Caleb. "He's yours. Humans and witches don't shift into animals."

"Okay, okay, you're right. I see your point. Just give me a second...I didn't even know it was possible. It appears that

I've been a father for the last...." He shrugged. "How old is he?"

"Twelve," Sherry answered. "And what do you mean, you didn't know it was possible?"

Caleb shrugged, then picked the cat up and placed him in his lap, stroking the soft fur. "I'm over four hundred years old. To my knowledge, I've never been a father before. I wonder why Celia didn't tell me?"

"We begged her to tell you," Sherry said, "but she said it wasn't safe. Why would she say something like that?"

"Not long before we broke up we were attacked. I killed the attacker, but she was never the same after that. She'd jump at every sound and seemed to be afraid all the time. I tried to calm her fears but she wouldn't listen. She kept insisting that they were still out there. Nothing I did or said was good enough anymore. She'd start a fight at the drop of a hat over nothing at all. A month or so later she said that she couldn't take it anymore and she told me not to call or come by." He sighed heavily. "I was tired of the fighting. I loved her, but I thought she didn't love me anymore. I guess my pride was hurt, I don't know. I did what she asked and left her alone and tried to forget." He cuddled the cat and rubbed his face over the top of his head. "Had I known about the child, I wouldn't have allowed her to have her way. I would have demanded to be in their lives."

"Shadow...I mean Mica." Sherry said. He lifted his head and made eye contact. "Follow me to that doorway. I'll bring your new clothes. You need to phase back now."

Mica leaped out of Caleb's lap and waited patiently on Sherry, then he followed her across the room.

Caleb watched them leave. "He seems to listen pretty well."

"He's a good kid," Sherry said from across the room. "He needs his father."

Caleb stood and approached Mica. "Hey, buddy, I'm gonna need your help. We need to track these guys down before they get away. Celia deserved better than that."

Desiree interjected. "Caleb, Celia died two years ago."

He raked his fingers through his hair. "Two years ago? I don't understand. Why am I just now hearing about all this?"

"For starters, we didn't know who you were," Sherry said as she joined the group again. "Young Mica here has been living as my cat, Shadow, for the last two years. I had no idea." She ruffled Mica's hair. "Drake recognized him as a shape shifter this morning, and patched together all the missing pieces of the story."

"Thank you for taking such good care of him, and I am sorry for the way I treated you earlier. It was uncalled for."

Sherry smiled. "Apology accepted. I know what a shock this is, and believe me, I was shocked this morning too. He's been through a lot in his young life. I've told him that I will always be there for him, and I will, but he needs a father—his father—and—"

"I want my son."

She felt Mica relax at her side, and she squeezed his shoulders. "Good. He needed to hear that from you, Caleb. He was so afraid that you wouldn't."

Caleb reached his hand out and grabbed the boy, pulling him into a bear hug. "I'm sorry. I'm sorry for everything, Mica. I've been livin' solo for so many years, it'll take some time to adjust. You'll have to be patient with your 'old man.' I've never had to do the father thing before, and you're half-grown. I'm getting a late start."

The boy hugged him back. "What do you want me to call you?"

"I'll answer to most anything, but I'd like for you to call me dad."

"So the mangy cat does have a heart," Drake said.

Caleb took a deep breath, then reluctantly looked to Drake. They had never seen eye to eye on anything. He kept his son in a hug and stuck his hand out to Drake. "I know that we've never gotten along...thank you, sire, for this."

Drake kept his face sober. "That had to hurt."

"It did."

Mica laughed and slapped Caleb on the back.

Chapter Fourteen

Drake placed an amulet in Sean's hand. "Follow them, and do not let them out of your sight."

Sean fastened the heavy gold chain around his neck. "Is there anything that I'm not supposed to let them do?"

Drake considered the question. He knew that Sherry wasn't going to be very happy to learn that she had a bodyguard following her around, but she had to be protected. He and Mica were stuck at the warehouse with a few issues that needed to be dealt with immediately or he'd be with her himself. He looked to Mica and Mica shook his head. "No, they are free to move about as they wish—for now anyway. I just need you to keep an eye out for Hargrove's son."

Sean bowed to Drake. "As you wish, sire, I will protect the queen...." He stole a glance at Mica. Mica's cold glare had him amend his sentence. "And the witch, with my life."

"Then go."

Sean bowed again and left, closing Drake's chamber door behind him.

Mica stared hard at the closed door and grumbled, "I don't trust that little weasel.

"Drop it, Mica. I know you two have issues, but—"

"He is insolent and disrespectful."

Karen Fuller

"But he is loyal to me and will do as he's told. We have other, more pressing, matters to discuss than your disdain for my bodyguard."

"If he allows harm to come to my mate, I will kill him."

"Noted. Now for the next topic—Caleb." Drake motioned for Mica to be seated.

Mica sat down in the chair and let out a collected breath, then glared at Drake. "What about him?"

Drake took a seat on his throne. "Sherry is fond of the boy."

Mica nodded. "Desiree is too."

"I've never pressed the issue. I know it's been three hundred years, but I need to know what happened with Caleb and his pack."

"That's Caleb's business, you should have asked *him*."

Drake folded his arms across his chest. "I'm asking *you*."

Mica raked his fingers through his hair in frustration. "I swore to him that I'd never speak of it."

"It's a little late now. The trouble has followed him here, onto our turf, and it has suddenly become *my* problem. We also have our own conflicts to worry about; Santana and his clan could be heading here as we speak. He has made it no secret that he wants control of New Orleans. I'll be damned if I'm gonna lose this war because I was kept ignorant of the details of Caleb's fuckup in England. Now, here's what I *do* know. He was nearly dead when you brought him back that day. What I don't know is the details."

Drake watched the muscles in Mica's jaw tense. He didn't want to have to order Mica to tell him, but he would if he had to.

"Okay, you already know some of it anyway. You might as well know the rest."

Drake frowned. "I do?"

Mica nodded. "You remember the other night when we arrived back from Tennessee?"

Drake gave him a puzzled look. "What does Tennessee have to do with it?"

"Caleb has a compulsive disorder. When he gets a thought in his head that he wants something...well, he becomes obsessed with it until he just takes what he wants, or attempts to anyway."

Drake rubbed the tension from the back of his neck. "Are you referring to the issue you had with him and Desiree?"

Mica nodded. "Yeah."

"So let me guess, he went after someone's mate."

Mica nodded again. "Yes, he gets it into his head that they want him too."

"Whose mate did he go after?"

"The alpha's." Drake rolled his eyes and shook his head as Mica continued. "He stole her away for several days, against her will I might add. When they caught up with him it wasn't pretty. I wasn't far behind. I had tracked him there as well. When I arrived they were getting ready to cut out his heart. I couldn't let them do that. He had saved my neck more than once in the vampire wars...I had to save him. You saw the shape he was in. I had to kill the alpha to rescue him."

Drake stroked his chin in thought. "I wonder why they would wait three hundred years to avenge their alpha."

"I don't know, but if they're after Caleb, they're after me too. After all, I'm the one that killed their alpha."

Drake shot Mica an irritated look. "That thought crossed my mind too. Yours and Caleb's actions have left me with no choice."

Mica cocked an eyebrow. "Your meaning?"

"Call Caleb, tell him to pack a bag for himself and pick up a few things for the boy. They'll be our guests until this is over."

Mica shook his head. "I don't think Caleb would want—"

"At this point I don't give a fuck what Caleb does or doesn't want. He is living in my domain, and will do as he's told. It seems that they were going after the boy to get to Caleb. I could feel Sherry's attachment to the boy. I don't want her getting hurt. I would imagine that you would have the same concerns for Desiree as well."

"Yes, but—"

"I'm not finished."

Mica gave Drake a cold glare. "Why do I get the feeling that I'm not going to like this?"

***

"Drake knew that I wanted to talk to him, and he's avoiding me. That's the only reason I can think of that he and Mica took off so fast," Sherry said to Desiree as she eased into the chair at the diner.

"Mica just said that there was some unfinished business that they had to take care of from a couple of days ago. He didn't act like it was a big deal to me, but he did say that it had to be resolved today," Desiree said.

"Sure," Sherry said as she studied the menu. "I personally think that it's an excuse."

Desiree smirked. "Trouble already?"

Sherry turned her head and saw the waitress approaching the table. "I'll tell you in a minute."

A young, pretty blond approached the table. She wore blue jeans, an orange t-shirt that read 'Eat at Joe's,' and had on a short, black apron tied at her hips. She smiled and said, "What can I get y'all to drink?"

Sherry smiled back at the waitress. "I'll have tea." She saw Desiree nod. "Make it two teas."

The girl pulled her order pad from her apron pocket and scribbled down two teas. She tapped the pen on her pad, then looked over her shoulder. When she looked back the smile had disappeared. She hesitated, then spoke. "Do either of you ladies know that guy in the booth over there?"

Desiree looked past her and saw Sean sitting in a booth across the room staring at their table. Frowning, she said, "Yeah, we know him."

The waitress let out a relieved breath, her smile returned. "Good. He's just been staring so intently at y'all that I was afraid we had a stalker situation going on. He's gorgeous, but his look is so intense that he's kinda scary."

Desiree shrugged, then glanced over at Sean again as she spoke to the waitress. "We're fine. He won't bother us."

"Okay, I'll take your word for it. Are y'all ready to order now or do you need more time?"

Sherry folded the menu and handed it to the waitress. "I'll have the turkey bacon club."

Desiree handed the waitress her menu as well. "Cheeseburger, well done, with the seasoned fries."

"Great! I'll place your ticket and be right back with the teas." She left and returned almost immediately with the teas, placing them in front of Sherry and Desiree. "I'll be back in a few minutes with your lunch."

Desiree took a sip of her tea then said, "You were saying?"

Sherry glanced at Sean again then back to Desiree. "Wait, are you just going to let this go?"

Desiree shrugged. "I'm sure Drake sent Sean to watch over us. I'd really be pissed if we hadn't already been kidnapped from this very diner yesterday." She shrugged again. "Hargrove is still out there. Maybe it's for the best…at least for now."

"I see your point, but I still don't like it."

"Me either, but hey, I like breathing too."

Sherry smiled. "Yeah, breathing's good."

Desiree laughed. "You're killing me. I need you to finish telling me why you think that Drake is avoiding you, because from my standpoint he is doing anything but."

Sherry looked away, toying with her glass. "Things were going great until we arrived at the warehouse."

"And?"

Sherry shrugged then glanced back at her friend. "It all started when he heard my thoughts and answered me in my head."

Desiree worried her bottom lip with her teeth. She winced then said, "Go on."

"All of a sudden everyone is calling me a queen. It was kinda fun when *he* did it, but when everyone else is doing it, it's kinda creepy." She sighed. "I demanded that he tell me what's going on, and he just said that we'd talk later. I thought when Caleb and little Mica left that he'd talk to me, but he had something else on his mind and…here we are."

"Honey, I need to ask you something really personal, and I don't want you to get mad, but it's important."

"Okay." She picked up her tea and took in a mouthful.

"What are your feelings for Drake?" Sherry nearly spewed the tea. She coughed a couple of times, then opened her mouth to object to the question, but Desiree held up her hand and continued. "I'm not askin' to be nosey. We're past the point of warnings. You're in too deep now."

"Now you're starting to scare me."

A tear slipped out of the corner of Desiree's eye. "I wish I had been successful in scaring you away yesterday morning, but fate had other plans, and now it's too late."

"Too late for what?"

"For you to leave and live a normal life."

Sherry gave her a weak smile. "Des, I have no intensions of leaving. I'm happy with my life the way it is at the moment. As for being normal…well, to tell the truth, there is *nothing* normal about either of us. I'd accepted that a long time ago. I thought you had too."

Desiree sniffed, then smiled a little. "You're right, we're not normal. I gave up being normal a hundred years ago. What is normal anyway, right?"

Sherry nodded. "Right."

The smile left Desiree's face as she searched Sherry's eyes. "Damn it, it's still nagging at me. I feel it in my gut that you're just trying to make me feel better."

Sherry huffed out a frustrated breath. "Des…look, what I *need* most from you is for you to stop this. I can read your *pity* for me in your expression, and to tell the truth it's starting to piss me off."

"I don't pity you, I—"

"Let me finish. I'm so happy and proud for you that you have finally found a great guy. Yes, being a vampire is a huge issue to overcome, but like I said before, we're not normal either. The short time I've been around you two as a couple I can see that he loves you very much. And if I'm correct in my assumptions, you love him too."

"Yes, but—"

Sherry threw up her hands. "But what?"

"We're talking about *you* and Drake, not *me* and Mica."

"You know something? I could choke you right now."

Desiree threw out her hands. "What?"

115

"I thought you were supposed to be my friend."

"Sherry, I *am* your friend. I love you as a sister. I'm just trying to protect—"

Sherry shook her head. "Don't you get it? I don't need you to protect me. What I need from you is your support. Stop feeling sorry for me and be happy for me. Please, just let me feel a small fraction of what you feel without the guilt."

"Guilt?"

"Yeah, I kinda feel guilty for wanting to be with Drake because I know that you don't approve."

"But with Drake?"

"Des, I know you don't like him, but—"

"It's not that I don't like him Sher; he's dangerous."

"And Mica's not? Besides, a little danger adds spice to your life. It keeps things exciting."

"I think that this kind of life might be a little more excitement that you're prepared for."

Sherry smiled. "I've had more excitement in the last two days than I've had in my entire life. It made me realize how dull and boring my existence has been so far. Drake makes me feel things that I've never felt before."

"Sher, they have a word for that. It's called lust."

The waitress set the plates down on the table. Desiree waved her on.

Sherry felt the heat flood her face. She knew that the girl had to have heard at least Desiree's comment. "I won't deny that I felt that from the moment I laid eyes on him. It's more than that, Des. Is it love? I don't know. I've never been in love before, but I know that I care for him deeply and I think he cares for me too."

"Sher, I know that you don't like me calling you naive," Sherry frowned. "But you are clueless about Drake's feelings for you."

"Okay, wise one, enlighten me," she said sarcastically. "If you know so much, then tell me how Drake really feels about me."

"He more than cares deeply for you."

"And you would know this, how? Has he said something to Mica?"

Desiree shook her head and took a small bite of her cheeseburger, chewing it thoughtfully before she spoke again. "He didn't have to. Everyone knows. Everyone but you, apparently."

Sherry shrugged. "You've lost me."

Desiree put her cheeseburger down and reached across the table, placing her hand over Sherry's. "He's claimed you as his mate."

Sherry's mouth gaped in stunned silence.

"You carry his mark. That's why you've heard all the 'queen' remarks today. You are their queen now. And I guess, since I am Mica's mate, that makes you my queen too. This is why *I* feel guilty, and why I said it's too late."

"But...how?" she sputtered.

"Don't feel bad. When Mica marked me I was clueless too. I found out when Caleb went into a rage and nearly killed me because of it. The others can sense it." She squeezed her hand. "Eat your lunch. I have a feeling that you're going to need all the strength you can get for what lies ahead."

Karen Fuller

118

Chapter Fifteen

Mica took out his cell phone and called Caleb.

"Hello?"

"Hello, Caleb."

"Did we forget something? We haven't even made it home yet."

"Uh, you and the boy need to come back to the warehouse. Drake's insisting, if you get my drift. He said to bring whatever you'll need for a few days, and stop somewhere and pick the boy up some things too."

"You're kidding, right?"

"Afraid not."

"We just left. The boy hasn't even seen where he's gonna live yet. Can't this wait a day or two?"

"It's not a request, Caleb."

"Damn it, Mica! Where the fuck does Drake come off giving me an order?"

"That's a rhetorical question."

Caleb sighed into the phone. "I know. I know. I'm just venting. Can you at least tell me why?"

"He thinks your pack is going to target the boy next to get to you."

"I can protect my son. Why would he care anyway, we're not vamps?"

"Drake's queen is fond of the boy, so is Desiree. He doesn't want to see her hurt."

"About that…since when does Drake have a queen? All the years I've known him he hasn't had a mate."

"It was a bit of a surprise to me too. I never figured he'd take a human for a mate."

"You did."

"I know."

"No offense, Mica, but—"

"Caleb, you're objecting like you have a choice. You don't and you know it."

"I know, don't remind me. But I will add that no one said I had to be happy about it."

"Keep it to yourself, and don't let Drake hear you. By the way, there is another reason for you to be here."

"Oh?"

"We've received word that Santana's clan may be trying to overthrow Drake's rule for New Orleans. We need everyone close by just in case."

"Another vampire war. Hmmm…New Orleans has never seen a vampire war. This could get ugly. But a good fight could make my forced confinement worthwhile. Does that mean you too?"

"Yeah."

"Does Dez know yet?"

"She and the queen went out, so, no, she doesn't know yet."

Caleb laughed into the receiver. "Dez is gonna be pissed."

"Yeah, I know."

***

Desiree sighed. "Sher, you haven't said a word in the last twenty minutes and only picked at your lunch. I know how you must feel—"

Sherry's mouth gaped. "You know how I feel?" she interjected. "I'm numb, so please tell me."

"I know you're depressed, but—"

"Depressed? What do I have to be depressed about?" She laughed and Desiree saw the fury in her eyes. "I just found out that I'm the fucking queen of the vampires, and I'm supposed to be depressed?" she nearly shouted.

"Keep your voice down." Desiree glanced around the room and saw Sean glaring. "People will hear you."

Sherry scowled. "Do you think I care if people hear me?"

"Sherry, please calm down,"

Sean rose from the booth and approached their table. "It's time to go."

"Go?" She glared at Sean. "Go where?"

"It is time to take you back, sire."

She laughed mechanically. "Sire—you know that's really funny, fucking hilarious in fact."

Desiree was worried now. "Come on, Sher, he's right. We need to go."

"Go? With you?" She laughed again. "I don't know where I'm going, but it certainly isn't with either of you."

"You're coming with me," Sean said calmly.

Sherry slid out of the chair and took a few steps back. "Like hell I am. Tell Drake he can kiss my a—"

"Sleep." Sean interjected as he locked eyes with her. Sherry dropped into his arms. His cell phone rang as he hoisted her over his shoulder.

Desiree's mouth gaped. "What did you do to her?"

"She's in thrall," he said as he fished his phone out of his pocket and answered it.

"Yes, sire…Your queen is unharmed, just unconscious… She was causing a scene and refused to return." Sean glanced around the room. "As you wish, we are on our way." The cell phone snapped shut.

He shifted Sherry's weight on his shoulder then nodded to Desiree. "Drake said we need to return now."

***

Sherry rolled over and snuggled closer to the warmth as she felt the cold prickly gooseflesh travel across her bare skin. In the dark, her hands felt around behind her for the covers and found none. Reaching out in front, her hands brushed across smooth hard abs. She yanked her hands back as if burned. *Oh God, there's someone in bed with me*, her mind screamed. *Where are my clothes?* Her eyes flew open, but the pitch-black in the room made it impossible to see, adding to the fear gripping her heart. She had no idea where she was or how she got there. In that split second panic settled in. *Run.* Her heart hammered in her chest as she tried to scramble away, and strong hands pulled her back. "Drake?" she squeaked.

"Yes, vixen," he said, pulling her across his chest and then wrapping his arms around her. He brushed his lips across her forehead as he spoke. "Calm your fears, it is only me."

The deep, familiar, rumble of his voice washed over her, and a sense of peace calmed her soul as she relaxed in his arms. "Thank God…I can't see…it's too dark in here. I woke up not knowing where I am, how I got here, or *who* I suddenly found myself in bed with. I was praying it was you. I think the shock took a couple years off my life."

"You are safe," he said. "and where you belong."

"Where are we? I'm cold." She felt him shift and a soft comforter slid across them both. "Thank you."

"You are in our chamber."

"I don't remember how I got here."

He sighed deeply. "According to Sean you were trying to run from me." She heard the sadness in his voice and it clutched at her heart. "He put you into a deep sleep and returned you to me." His statements touched the very root of her fear, her loss of choice.

"So...you forced me back here. We need to talk."

"I do what must be done. You belong with me."

"I don't have a say in all this?"

"You do, but the Fates have made their decision. Our ways and laws are as old as the threads of time and we are bound by them. The rules of our race allow us only one mate in a lifetime, and since we are immortal the choice of the mate is determined by the Fates. You were chosen at the time of your birth to be my mate."

"Come on, Drake. You can't tell me that you really believe all that crap. The year is two thousand and eleven, not seventeen eleven. Look at us. Look at yourself. You are perfect and I am...not. I am just me, plain ole Sherry."

"I do not know why you always try to belittle yourself to me. I see you as a strong, desirable woman, worthy to be my queen and rule beside me. And yes, I do believe it. I know it to be true. You are the one that the Fates have chosen for me, and you are perfect to me."

"How do you know, Drake? How do you know that I am *the one*? I mean, it just doesn't make sense to me. I am very fond of you and you are very important to me. I definitely can't deny the attraction to you. I just don't see why you chose me. I'm nothing special. I'm afraid that one day I'll wake up to find you gone because you finally realized that I'm a nobody."

"You were never a nobody, little one. You are my chosen queen. But to answer your question, I know because we recognize our mates for the first time, not by face, but by scent. I knew the moment I crossed Mica's threshold and caught your scent that I had found my mate. I consider myself very fortunate that you are beautiful as well."

"But I'm not, and someday soon you will see it."

"You are."

"Okay, okay, for arguments sake I am…passable, I guess. What if I hadn't been? If I had been ugly—"

"Your appearance wouldn't have mattered, because the scents of our mates drive us to the point of obsession. I would have still claimed you…I would have had no choice. Our primal instinct takes over, and I wouldn't have been able to fight it."

She scoffed. "I find that hard to believe."

"I don't *want* to fight it, vixen."

"I still don't get it."

"Sherry—"

"I'm not trying to argue, Drake, I'm trying to understand. As I said before, I'm just me. I'm nothing special. You claim that you think I'm beautiful—"

"You are," he interjected.

"Let me finish. But then you claim looks have nothing to do with it. Well, if it's not looks, then what is it?"

"It only took a small taste of your blood to confirm the signs and seal the bond. Your blood sings to me, little one, it sings to my soul. Its siren's call drives me to the point of irrational thoughts. You are now mine forever, as I am now forever and always yours."

"Forever?"

"Yes; through our bond I will always sense where you are, what you're feeling, and when I wish I will be able to read your thoughts. Once you've tasted my blood then you'll be able to do the same. Our souls are now linked in such a way that we need each other to survive."

"What do you mean, that we need each other to survive?"

"A vampire cannot survive without their mate. If one dies, the other soon follows."

"So, the only reason I'm here now is because you can't survive without me."

Drake sighed heavily. "For reasons I cannot fathom, you do not deem yourself worthy of love. Although love is not a requirement for mated pairs, you are here now because I love you and cannot survive without you."

Her heart raced. *He loves me?*

"I have loved you from the moment our eyes met."

The darkness of the room was beginning to get on her nerves. She heard the candor in his voice, but wanted to see the sincerity in his eyes. Her heart wanted to believe him, but the years of being shunned by society for what she was had left its mark. Trust in another didn't come easy to her. "You can't love me. We haven't known each other long enough, and for the record there is no such thing as love at first sight." She felt Drake shift and slightly pull away.

"Come here, vixen."

"What are you doing?"

"I'm going to convince you of how I really feel."

"How are you gonna do that?"

"Through our ways…vampire ways."

"Huh?"

"You only need a small taste of my blood to seal the mental bond between us. The physical bond is already there."

"I don't…I mean…will it…ugh! Damn it, Sherry, just spit out a simple question." She heard him laugh softly and smacked his arm playfully. "Stop laughing at me."

"I will try. I already know your question because I can hear your mind screaming it through our bond. I will allow you the opportunity to voice it."

"I'm not saying that I believe all that you're telling me. I know you don't lie; we've been through that one. I do trust that you believe what you are saying is true. I want to know, if I try what you are suggesting, will it change me? Will I become one of you?"

"You are already one of us."

She took a sharp intake of breath. *What? How?*

"You are my mate, vixen, that makes you one of us; but no, you are not a vampire, and tasting my blood will not make you one."

Relieved, she expelled her breath slowly. "Okay, convince me."

He nipped at the sensitive spot at the nape of her neck, sending a ripple of need through her. "For our kind, mates typically exchange blood during sex."

She sighed, snuggling closer, giving in to the intoxicating feelings, and felt herself grow wet. "Mmmm, go on."

She heard the slight amusement in his voice as he continued. "It is a highly...erotic and a very addicting experience," he said as he guided her hand to his engorged cock.

Keep laughing, sire, she thought. *I may be new to this, but I will make you pay.* She ran her fingers over the silken member, and with the other hand touched herself, aching at the mere thought of riding him hard and fast. His cock grew harder beneath her touch. She ran her hand down the length of him, rolling the heavy sack between her fingers, then back up to tease the head. *I will make you ache for me as badly as I do for you.*

"I'm not laughing at you, love, but I don't believe that I'll ever tire of your sense of humor. I enjoy your...eagerness. I can hear your thoughts, vixen, and for the record, I already do. You are playing with fire, teasing me with those thoughts."

She smiled, knowing full well he couldn't see her in the dark. "Good." She didn't really believe he could read her thoughts, although he was right on the mark about what she had been thinking. She sat up, then draped her leg across his body, straddling him. Growing bolder with his approving growl, she rocked herself seductively over the tip of his cock. "Erotic and addicting, huh?"

He hissed out a "Yesss" as he thrust his hips up.

She backed up just out of his reach. "Uh uh, no, I don't think so, sire. If you're trying to convince me, we're doing this my way. If I want to take my time and tease you first, I will. You will wait until I am ready." A low growl rumbled from his chest and she laughed. "*My* way, sire."

The amusement returned to his voice. "Are you giving an order to your king?"

"Yes, I—"

He pulled her down and covered her mouth with his, cutting off her response. His tongue slipped between her parted lips, plunging deeply, stroking hers. He ran his hands across her hips to her ass, then slipped two fingers into her liquid heat.

She moaned and swayed into his hand, the need for more coiling in the pit of her belly.

His lips left hers to travel along her neck as his fingers continued to plunge deeper with each stroke. He said, "You were saying?"

"You, sire, don't play fair," she said as she sat up and stilled his hands, clasping them in front of her. "You cheated."

He laughed softly. "I didn't cheat. I'm just trying to maintain order in my kingdom and keep my queen happy at the same time."

She scoffed, "Yeah, right, like you really care whether I'm happy or not as long as you get your way."

Drake frowned. "Lights dim." The lights illuminated to a soft glow. He gazed into her eyes. "Why would you say something like that?"

She shrugged. "You are the king, and naturally you take what you want. At the moment you think you want me—"

"I think—"

"Yes, you have never taken my feelings into it. Never once have you asked me if I want any part of this life. This…." She threw out her hand then let it drop back to her side. "This forced confinement. And you think I should be happy about it."

"Yes, I have, and yes, I do."

She shook her head. "You have never asked—"

"I never had to."

Narrowing her eyes, she said, "Why, because you're king and that makes you exempt somehow?"

"No, love, I'm not *that* self-centered." She sputtered and he continued before she could respond. "I've known what you're thinking and what you feel from the moment I took your blood."

She cocked an eyebrow and glared. "Care to tell me what I'm thinking *now*, sire?"

He smiled. "You're thinking that I'm a self-centered ass and a few other very descriptive words." Her eyes widened and his smile grew as he continued to read her mind. "You also love my—"

Oh my God, he's reading my mind. She felt the heat flood to her cheeks. "Okay, I believe you," she interjected before he could finish, and she was completely humiliated. She hadn't intended for her mind to stray to the luscious parts of his body. "You *can* read my mind."

"Yes, vixen, I can. And for the record, I am a vampire king, not a god."

You are to me, flitted through her mind before she could stop it.

He tilted his head and disengaged his hands from her tight grasp, then ran his hands up her body to cup her breasts. The nipples pebbled at his gaze and soft touch as he ran his thumbs over the heightened peaks. "I guess that makes you my goddess queen."

She took a quivering breath as need rippled through her body. Closing her eyes she savored the feelings. "I believe you—that you can read my mind, I mean. But my feelings? How can you know what I feel when I don't know myself?"

"Hummm, let me see...." He rolled her nipple between his fingers. "I sense your desire...." Her eyes flew open and she cocked an eyebrow. His smile returned. "And your irritation at me." The corners of her mouth turned up in a small smile. "You feel confused. Your heart wants to believe me, but your mind is filled with distrust." He frowned. "You've been hurt in the past, and don't feel yourself worthy of love." His eyes flashed red. "I will hunt this mortal down and rip his throat out for hurting you like that."

She caught her breath. "Drake, no!"

"He has hurt what is mine. He must pay."

Sherry reached out and caressed his face with her fingertips. "It was a long time ago. He's now just a bad memory and means nothing to me; please let it go at that."

"If he means nothing to you, then why—"

"Because he's human, and we're supposed to be civilized. We don't rip each other's throats out just because we can...or most of us don't anyway." He opened his mouth to object and she interjected, "I would feel guilty."

He expelled a long breath as his eyes turned back to blue. "I will spare him then. I will not have you feel that way."

"Thank you."

"It's time we rid you of your confusion and mistrust."

"I honestly don't see how. I've felt this way for a very long time. It's easier said than done."

"It is actually quite simple." His eyes locked with hers. "Complete the bond and you won't have to guess or doubt. You will know."

"What if I'm disappointed?"

"You won't be."

He looked sincere so she smiled. "My way?"

He laughed and hugged her to him.

Chapter Sixteen

She sat up next to him on her knees, and when he reached for her she said, "Do something with your hands. Place them behind your head or whatever, just don't touch me. I get too distracted when you touch me."

He placed his hands behind his head, interlocking his fingers. "As you wish, sire."

She smiled at his remark as she gazed at his body, his cock hardening under her stare.

"If you keep thinking those thoughts I won't be able to keep my hands to myself."

"You keep your hands where they are," she said as she reached out and wrapped her fingers around his cock. It grew, swelling further beneath her fingers. "My way, remember?" she said, then ran her tongue up the vein in his cock, starting at the base, up to the head. Pre-cum pooled at the tip.

She wrapped her lips around the head, taking his thick cock into her mouth. Bobbing her head as she took him deeper with every stroke of her tongue, her hand wrapped around the base. Her own need coiled between her thighs.

He growled his approval as his hips surged with her movements. "A little faster, vixen. Yes, that's right." He made a move to unlace his fingers, then thought better of it when she paused and cut her eyes at him. "Since you won't let me touch you, let me watch you touch yourself."

She nodded once, then closed her eyes and continued. With the other hand she reached between her legs and rubbed herself. She felt the wetness beneath her fingers, and just the thought of him watching her made her ache more.

"Spread your legs a little further and insert a couple of fingers." She spread her legs further, slipping two fingers between her folds, brushing the swollen nub as she did. "Deeper, love, pleasure yourself while I watch you."

Her inner walls clenched around her fingers, plunging deep as he watched, keeping rhythm to her mouth taking in his cock. She felt the peak build with each movement.

"You are so wet. Cum for me love. I want to watch your body clench around your fingers as you cum for me."

She did as he commanded and a million sensations pulsed through her body as she plunged her fingers in as far as they would go for him. Her juices dripped across the back of her hand.

He roared out his release as he thrust one final time, coming down her throat.

She released her hold on his still semi erect cock, then laid her head down on his thigh. She remained on her knees, spent, as her body's pulsations gradually slowed.

***

As Drake gazed at her wet curls, the scent of her arousal filled his nose, and he felt his erection swell again fully. He had agreed to let her have it her way, but her way was about to kill him. He wanted to bury himself deep inside her. "May I touch you now, sire?"

She turned her head and grinned. "Yes, you may, sire."

He moved so fast she squealed when he flipped her over onto her back and covered her body with his. "That was the

132

sexiest thing I've ever witnessed, and I will never underestimate the talent of this beautiful mouth," he said, then devoured her mouth with his, plunging inside and tasting himself on her tongue. He broke the kiss and stared intently into her eyes. "I'm not near finished with you yet, vixen."

She looked up at him as the corners of her mouth turned up into a smile.

"My turn," was all he said as he rolled over toward the nightstand and then back with a dagger suddenly in his hand.

Her eyes rounded. "What are you going to do with that?"

"When the time is right, I'm going to place a small cut here." He pointed to the soft spot on his neck, near the shoulder, then he placed the dagger next to her pillow. "It only takes a small taste to seal the bond."

She grimaced as she looked at the dagger then back at him.

He brushed his fingers along the side of her face in a tender caress then placed a soft kiss on her lips. "It's not as bad as you're thinking, love." Through their bond he felt her fear. He had hoped that the non-demanding kiss would relax her, and it had some, but if she didn't trust him this would never work. He needed her trust to complete the connection between them; his soul craved it. "Remember when I took your blood this morning?"

She nodded. "Yes."

"What did you feel?"

She hesitated as she thought about it. "I felt…." A trace of a smile graced her lips as she remembered and her body relaxed beneath him. "Actually it was kind of…erotic. I thought it would hurt, but it was a little euphoric instead."

"That's just a small taste of what you'll feel again, love, only this time it will be stronger because you'll be feeling what I feel too."

She looked into his eyes and came to a decision. "I'll make a deal with you, Drake. You'll have to agree or I'm not going through with this. It would kill me to walk away from you, but it's all or nothing."

"I really don't see where either of us has a choice, but…your terms?"

"*If* what you say is true and I can see through the bond that connection that you say is there is actually there. *And* that you are truly sincere with your thoughts and feelings, then…well…I'll remain by your side in whatever capacity you want. I'm not one hundred percent sure of the feelings I have for you other than I want to jump in bed with you whenever we're alone for longer than two minutes. I know that I care for you a great deal, and I can tell you that I have never cared this much for anyone before; you have grown very important to me. The last thing in the world I would want to do to you is hurt you, but love? I've never been 'in love' before so I'm not really sure what I'm feeling."

"So far what you've said is agreeable," he said then smiled, and humor laced his voice. "And I find no objections to you jumping in bed with me every time we're alone." Returning his smile, the blood rushed to her cheeks. "So far you haven't said anything negative that we have to bargain for, so there must be a 'but' in there somewhere."

"*But,* if I don't see that you're sincere and I feel like you're just stringing me along…well…it would kill me, but I'd be out of here and I'd expect you to allow me to leave. No strings attached."

"Agreed."

Her mouth gaped. "No arguments?"

He placed his finger under her chin, closing her mouth, then kissed the tip of her nose. "No."

"You're either overly confident or don't care if I leave. Which is it?"

"Neither. I know exactly how I feel about you, and based on what you said, you'll be with me for eternity as my queen. I'm not going to argue with that, love, so yes, I agree."

"About that…you've mentioned eternity several times now, and—"

"Don't worry about the eternity issue. I hear your questions, but I don't have all the answers yet."

"But Drake, I'm human…I won't live—"

"The Fates have planned this from your birth. The sisters can have a wicked sense of humor, but somehow, some way, you will be immortal and by my side."

"How do you know? I mean, you are putting a lot of faith in legends. Why do you believe so strongly?"

He kissed her forehead. "I have met the sisters and they told me of my destiny, *and* that I would rule for eternity."

She searched his eyes. "When?"

"Three hundred years ago, when I was still human, I lost my wife to childbirth. I never got to know my unborn son. Everything had been stripped from me. I was alone and had no desire to continue living, so I lost myself in the bottle."

"It must have been awful." Her voice caught, and a tear trailed down her cheek. "I'm sorry."

"A few days after they died I drank myself into a drunken stupor. I woke three days later, in a dark barn, covered in my own blood and vomit, with the stink of the livestock surrounding me. My life as I knew it was over. I somehow knew that I was alive, but not. A feral rage now consumed me…I was lethal and ravenous. Life, human or otherwise, meant little to me. I had nothing left to hold on to my humanity. The lust for blood was all I cared about. Instinctively the only thing I feared was the sunlight.

135

"My sire was Reginald Loxley. At the command of the Fates he took advantage of my drunken state, and was ordered to convert me rather than end my pitiful life. He left me to wreak whatever havoc a newborn could inflict on an unsuspecting society. He was reputed to be a rogue, an outlaw, and as vicious as they come. He cared for no one but himself. I'm surprised he managed to follow orders. When a vampire sires another, we are supposed to be responsible for our progeny, but Reginald didn't stick around long enough to even see if I survived the conversion.

"The city of London was spread before me like the finest feast at the tables in the king's castle. Some bloke's horse fell victim to my cravings, but the taste of its blood only whetted my appetite. I was prepared to take London by storm, but when I stepped out of the stall the sisters were there, waiting for me. They were hags really, old and haggard, but they commanded a power, a power that couldn't be ignored. I initially had a mind to devour them and set out for London, but they laughed when I fought their invisible wall, and proceeded to tell me of their plans for me and what my future held. They laid their hands on me and calmed my uncontrollable bloodlust. Oh, I still craved blood, but I was now able to control the cravings and only took what I needed to survive and thrive.

"For five years I was their tool of destruction. They commanded me to convert my friend, Mica, and build an army, and so the vampire wars began. The fighting took place in the black of night. Any human that was unfortunate enough to be caught out in those late hours we either converted or drained. Our armies inflicted mayhem on the unsuspecting city. The death tolls, both vampire and human, mounted until the hags were satisfied. Then, as suddenly as they began, the wars were over, and peace once again reigned over London.

"It was now the year 1720. Had I remained human I would have been thirty. At the time of my conversion I was twenty-five, and so I will remain for eternity. The sisters took me aside, and as a reward for my loyalty told me to set sail for the Americas. The country was young and our kind hadn't established a foothold there yet. I was to take my first progeny, Mica, with me and reign as king over my territory. I was told to build an army and rule my subjects with an iron fist and little leniency, because when my mate was sent to me it would trigger a vampire war that would put London to shame, and I would need every able body loyal to my command. I've had word that there is unrest in the Texas clans and they seek my territory. That was the first sign that I would find you. The hags also said that I would be betrayed by someone close to me, and to hold those I considered dear closer to me. Am I protective of you? Yes, love, I am, because I know what lies ahead. The future is set, but not written in stone. My enemies would use you like a weapon against me."

Karen Fuller

Chapter Seventeen

He has overcome so much, she thought as a few more tears coursed down her cheeks. She reached up and ran her fingertips down his face in a soft caress. "You've waited almost three hundred years for me?"

He leaned his cheek into her hand, then kissed her palm. "Yes, and I would have waited three hundred more if necessary." He then kissed the tears from her cheeks. "I wanted you to understand why you are so important to me."

"I'm sorry if my episode in the diner hurt you. For what it's worth, I believe you. I can hear the sincerity in your voice."

"But?"

She sighed heavily. "But...it's just...I don't know, Drake. It's like everything came down on top of me at once. Look at it from my perspective. One minute I'm myself, living my boring everyday life, wishing something exciting would happen. And in the blink of an eye the most gorgeous guy I've ever laid my eyes on walks into my life and takes me hostage. After he steals my innocence and introduces me to some of the most mind-blowing sex on this side of the planet, he tells me he loves me and we are to spend eternity together. I'm sorry, but that kind of stuff only happens in romance novels. It doesn't happen to me, and it just doesn't seem real.

It's like I dreamed you up and now I can't wake up. I'm afraid when I do wake up you'll be gone and I'll never be the same."

Drake sat up on his knees, the corners of his mouth turned up in a smile as he positioned himself between her legs.

From the soft glow of the bed lamp she saw the muscles in his massive chest flex and ripple as he positioned her legs over his shoulders. She watched him with fascination. His body, so god-like, was perfection. And the way he looked at her—his eyes smoldering and that sexy smile—sent a jolt of pure need through her body. *God, all he has to do is look at me and I want to jump him*, she thought, then smiled back coyly. "Obviously you aren't even listening to me. What are you doing?"

His smile grew as he slipped his hands beneath her hips, lifting her to his mouth. "I *heard* every word, vixen." She realized in that moment that he had evidently read her thoughts and felt the heat rise to her cheeks. "I'm going to prove to you that I'm not a figment of your imagination."

"You're wrong. You're the most elaborate dream I've ever h—" The words caught in her throat as his tongue glided across her slit and his mouth descended on her sensitive nub. Her inner walls clenched and her body jerked at the strong sensations his mouth created as he suckled and teased. She felt a couple of his fingers glide easily into her wetness and pump in and out to the rhythm of his mouth. Locking her ankles around his neck, she clutched his hair between her fingers, pulling him closer, panting and writhing beneath his lips. She whimpered his name as her whole body tensed and the climax hit her hard.

"That's it, love, cum for me," he said as he lowered her hips level with his cock. He placed his cock at her opening and penetrated just enough to submerge the head. She was wet, and her inner walls still pulsated from her recent climax. She opened her eyes and his gaze leveled with hers. His muscles were tense with restraint. "Tell me what you need."

"Need?"

Her eyes widened as he moved slightly, penetrating a little deeper, then pulling out again. "Tell me what you need from me."

"I need…." She paused. Her eyes left his to travel down his body, and stopped to stare where their bodies were partially joined. His muscles were taut, and what she could see of his cock was deep pink and swollen. She licked her lips and tried to move her hips a little closer to take him in. The ache to have him fill her was almost unbearable, but he remained unmovable. She looked back into his eyes. "You, all of you. Please, Drake, I need to feel you inside me. Please, make love to me."

Her eyes closed as she felt his hips shift forward, his cock filling her, probing deep. He wrapped her legs around his waist as he continued to plunge in and out of her tight sheath, her juices coating them both. Her body welcomed his as her inner walls clenched around his cock, milking him, pulling him deeper with each thrust. He shifted, slicing a small cut in his neck with the dagger, then grabbed her hips and picked up the pace. Her breath caught as she felt her body start to explode.

"Drink, love," he said. "Complete the bond."

As her body pulsated around his cock, she opened her mouth and placed her lips over the wound at his neck, letting his blood fill her mouth. He roared his approval as his own climax gripped him. He bit down on the soft spot on her neck, letting her blood fill his mouth and calm his soul.

Just as soon as she tasted his blood, her world burst in a multitude of sensations. Never feeling more alive, she felt his cock throbbing within her. She felt what he felt as the cum shot from his body and the first tastes of her blood hit his tongue. Her heart swelled as all his emotions and feelings washed over her. *My god*, she thought in wonder. *He does love me.*

Yes, I do.

Did I just read your mind?

Yes, love.

How cool is that?

She felt his body shake with laughter as he withdrew his fangs, sealing the small wounds with his tongue. "I will never grow bored with your innocent take on life."

***

Sherry sat up in the enormous bed, straining her eyes to see past the dim light coming from the lamp on the nightstand. The room was vast and appeared endless in the inky blackness just out of reach of the meager light. She glanced over at Drake. He was propped up against the headboard watching her reactions.

"There must be no moon tonight. It is so dark in here."

"There are no windows in this room, love." He nodded to her questioning look. "Vampire."

Her eyes widened at her own stupidity. "Since I've seen you in the sunshine I forgot that you have a problem with the sun." She glanced around at the darkness again. "With no windows or clocks of any kind that I can see, how do you tell what time it is?"

"Vampires sleep very little and have an internal clock. We can generally sense the time quite accurately. And since we're nocturnal we can see very well in the dark as well." He felt her apprehension. "I can feel your unease, love. I don't want you to feel that way here, especially in our chambers. I can get you a clock if it would make you feel more comfortable."

"Thank you."

He smiled. "A clock is a small concession on my part. As for the time, you weren't out long. I believe it's still afternoon."

She nodded then looked at him curiously. "Drake, something you said a few seconds ago doesn't make sense to me. You said that vampires sleep very little. I saw you sleep at my house—quite soundly I might add."

"That's the first good sleep I've had in ages. I believe I have you to thank for that."

"*Me*? What did I have to do with it?"

"After bonding with you, my soul was finally at peace. I've not really known peace in three hundred years. 'Lights,'" he said aloud and the room lit so brightly that Sherry had to close her eyes for a second to adjust. "The lights are on voice command. Right now they are programmed to my voice. We will have your voice commands added when you're ready."

Sherry rubbed her eyes, then looked around again. The darkness had made the room appear smaller than it actually was. In full light it carried the richness of a palace. The bed, where they sat, was on the back side of the room in the middle of the wall. To her right, the bathroom was incorporated into the room with a large shower with stone walls on one side and an oversized jetted tub on the other. The tub was surrounded by greenery and unlit candles. A doorway stood between the shower and the tub. Through the lit doorway she saw a long granite countertop adorned with custom double sinks and gold fixtures. She assumed, from her vantage point, that the toilet was across from the sink, just out of sight.

It is, he answered in her mind.

She raised an eyebrow as she looked over at him. "No walls?"

He shrugged. "I've never had the need for them. No one enters our chambers unless I allow them. Even then, few get this far back into the room unless it's being cleaned." He pointed to the long colorful drapes that hung separating the sleeping area from the rest of the room. They were tied back with golden cords. "Those curtains can be released if you feel a need for more privacy."

She nodded then looked to her left. She saw sliding doors that covered nearly the entire space. "What's behind those doors?"

"Our closet."

She leaned over and kissed his cheek, then snuggled against him. Her voice was laced with laughter. "You put clothes behind a door, but don't put walls around a bathroom?"

He smiled. "Yes...I've never questioned that logic until now. We can make changes if you wish it."

"No, love, what I've seen of the room is beautiful. I wouldn't want to change a thing...at least for now."

He hugged her tighter and kissed her forehead.

She closed her eyes to the feeling of his embrace. "I just felt your heart warm."

He tilted her chin up and kissed her lips gently, then looked into her eyes when the kiss broke. "You called me love."

"Yes." She bit her lip, waiting expectantly. "Do you mind?"

"No, not at all, vixen, I rather enjoy hearing it. Why the change of heart?"

"I felt what was in your heart when I tasted your blood. I know that you've been telling me your feelings all along, but I've had bad experiences with the male population. I can trust now that you will never hurt me."

"Are you trying to say that you love me?"

She shrugged, smiling sheepishly. "I know I've been obsessed with you from the beginning, which leads me to believe that I probably always have loved you. I'm sorry if I hurt you. I guess I put up a wall to keep from getting hurt, even denying my feelings to myself. I can be a bit stubborn sometimes."

He laughed as he hugged her tighter. "I am stubborn as well, so I'm sure we'll butt heads from time to time. But always remember what is in my heart."

She reached up and kissed his check. Humor laced in her voice. "I'll try to keep that in mind."

Karen Fuller

Chapter Eighteen

Sherry smoothed the bottom of her sweater over her hips, then looked at the closet again, shaking her head. She was a little miffed at Drake at the moment. Every piece of clothing she owned was hung neatly on the rack. The closet, her side, also held an assortment of very nice outfits in her size that she'd never seen before. The questions when and how bothered her more than she thought they should.

Drake had left the room an hour ago after Sean had knocked on the door, alerting him to something that was going on. He left, giving her a quick peck on the cheek with instructions on where the towels were and to be ready in an hour. He was gone before she could attempt to read his mind. Somehow she felt that was deliberate on his part. She had every intention of getting to the bottom of whatever was going on just as soon as she could find him.

Finding him, however, in this huge place might prove to be difficult.

She pulled her cell phone out of her back pocket and checked the time. It had been an hour. *I guess I'll have to go find him myself,* she thought as she headed for the door. When she reached for the doorknob a movement out of the corner of her eye caught her attention. Turning her head, she stared at the fireplace. The movement came from a small cage on the mantle. Curiosity at what kind of pet Drake would want to keep prompted her to investigate.

Sherry was about three steps away from the mantel when she realized the cage contained a huge rat. The rat stood on his hind legs with his front paws wrapped around the bars, staring at her with his red beady eyes, his whiskers twitching as if he were irritated. She felt the gooseflesh travel up her arms in revulsion. "Why in the hell would Drake want you for a pet?"

Who for a pet? she heard from out of nowhere.

She spun around, startled. "Drake?"

I'm on my way. Who are you talking to?

You just took about ten years off my life. Don't do that.

He opened the door and stepped inside. She could see his amused expression, which further grated her nerves. He nodded toward the cage. "I see you've met our prisoner."

The word 'prisoner' took her by surprise. "Prisoner?" she glanced at the rat again, then back at Drake. "That's not a pet?"

Drake laughed. "Not hardly. That, my love, is Jason Hargrove."

"The witch hunter."

"Yes."

Sherry shook her head, then shuddered in revulsion. "Desiree's good. I'll give her that. She told me she had turned him into a rat, but I guess I didn't take her words quite so literally."

"You're afraid of rats?"

She scrunched her nose then glared at the hairy beast before she answered. "Not afraid, per se...they're just disgusting, nasty creatures." Then she turned back, giving Drake a worried look. "Rats are nocturnal?"

He nodded once. "Yes."

"He can *see* in the dark." Drake nodded again. "Oh my God, Drake!" She jabbed her finger at the cage. "He watched us." She felt the blood rush to burn her cheeks. "He watched me!"

Drake frowned. "These chambers are large, love. I doubt he has the ability to see that far."

She plopped down in a nearby chair and covered her face in her hands. "I don't believe that."

He knelt down and pulled her hands away, then cupped her face in his hands, placing a soft kiss on her lips. "I do, love."

She refused to let the subject go. "Well, I'm sure he's not deaf. Sound carries in a large room like this, and we weren't quiet by any means." He shook his head in a placating manner, so she continued quickly. "You also told me many things that I'm sure you would prefer to keep between us, a secret."

His jaw clenched in anger at himself when her words sunk in. He stood abruptly, then snatched the cage from the mantel, causing the rat to squeal in terror. "*Sean*," he roared. Sherry jumped at the outburst.

The door flew open, and Sean rushed in. "Sire?"

Drake shoved the cage at Sean. "Do something with Hargrove." When Sean took the cage and gave him a questioning look, he continued. "Put him with the rest of the prisoners."

Sean bowed. "Yes, sire." He left the room, closing the door behind him.

Sherry rose from the chair and approached Drake. She smiled, then caressed her fingers lightly down his cheek and felt him relax under her touch. "Thank you."

He pulled her to him and gave her a long leisurely kiss that left her damp and breathless. "No, thank you. You are a true queen, worthy to rule beside me."

She smirked. "What did I do to bring that on?"

"I thought of him as a rat, not as a prisoner. It never crossed my mind that I shouldn't speak freely in front of him."

"Drake, he *is* just a rat."

"Yes, at the moment. But what if something happened and Desiree's spell was reversed and he escaped?"

"He would know all our secrets."

"Exactly."

"Knowing the enemy's secrets gives you the upper hand."

"Spoken like a true leader."

"It's hard to stay mad at you."

He cocked an eyebrow and looked into her eyes. "You're mad at me?"

"I'm a little put out, yes."

She felt him touch her mind. "Ah...you're wanting to know how and when I retrieved your possessions."

"Yes."

"You were busy with little Mica. You remember when I called Sean to come get us?" She nodded. "I also left instructions with Sean for Jacob and Tracy to remove your possessions after we left. I knew that you weren't going back there."

She frowned. "That was awfully presumptuous of you. Don't you think we should have discussed this first?"

"No, it was no longer safe for you there, love. We both have enemies, and now it seems Caleb's enemies as well. I couldn't take the chance that you'd get caught in the crossfire. You belong with me."

150

She pressed her lips in a thin line and glared. "You may be king, but if we're supposed to be partners, there are certain things that need to be discussed before you just—"

He smiled and kissed her forehead, pulling her to him. "Be patient with me, love. I *am* king, and I am not accustomed to discussing my decisions before acting on them. I've been ruling for three hundred years, give or take. It will be an adjustment for me as well, but I will try to remember to consider your feelings when dealing with issues that evolve around us."

She relaxed in his arms. "Thank you."

"We will be together for eternity. I don't want to spend the majority of it arguing with you. I'm sure we'll continue to have our disagreements, but I don't want to cause unnecessary ones."

"Drake, I saw my clothes and jewelry in the closet. Where are the rest of my things?"

"I had Jacob and Tracey move the rest of your things to our mansion just north of the bayou."

"You have a mansion?"

"*We* have a mansion."

She smiled. "I can't wait to see it."

"Soon. You'll have to wait a bit longer to see it. I can protect you better here. When this is over I'll take you there."

"As I said before, it's hard to stay mad at you."

"Good. I'll remind you of that later."

There was a knock at the door and she frowned, looking up at Drake. "Why, what's happening?"

"Later, love. I have business to attend to, and you need to meet your subjects."

She narrowed her eyes and glared, trying to read his mind, but he blocked her. "That's not fair, Drake. You're already pissing me off."

He opened the door. "In time you'll understand what I had to do."

She glanced up at him again as he ushered her out into the hallway. "Why, what did you do?"

He let out a long breath as they entered the main throne room. "Only what was necessary for a man in my position to maintain order."

A movement to her left caught her attention as two vampires drug a semi-conscious man to a long beam set up with hanging shackles. They secured the man's wrists and let him hang as his knees buckled from apparent despair. One of the vampires reached up and ripped the shirt from his back. The sound of shredding fabric filled the otherwise quiet room. From the man's size Sherry was pretty sure he was human and she thought he looked familiar, but didn't know from where.

It was obvious that he was about to be punished for some injustice. In alarm Sherry looked at all the sober faces around the room. She saw Mica and Desiree next to the throne. Mica's expression was resolved and unbending. Desiree was weeping openly, alarming Sherry further. "Drake," her voice shook. "What's going on?"

He led her to her throne next to his, encouraging her to sit. "I'm just maintaining order, love."

She searched his eyes, trying to understand. "I don't understand. Who is he? I can see he's human, but what did he do? Why is Desiree crying?" Her voice was barely a whisper.

You must remain strong, love. Others are watching. Her bottom lip quivered as she looked around the room. He continued in her mind. *He is Mica's driver, Charles.*

Her gaze snapped back to his. *Why, what did he do?*

He failed to follow orders, and left you and Desiree vulnerable to Justin Hargrove.

She mouthed a silent 'no' as the tears trickled down her cheeks.

I have to, love. Remember who I am. I am king, and I must enforce the consequences for failure to obey direct orders. I won't kill him, he will live, but neither will I show him leniency.

Why must Desiree and I witness this?

It is our way...every eye must witness the punishment and remember. Keep your chin up and shoulders back, love. Others will watch you for signs of weakness. You must not show any weakness, understand? We are warriors, and being strong will earn you their respect. You are my queen now. You are their queen now.

She let out a quivering breath, wiped the tears from her face and nodded. *I understand, and I will try.*

He gave her a trace of a smile before he turned and faced his clan. She watched him stride to the center of the throne room. He held out his right hand and a Cat o' Nine Tails was placed in his grasp. The whip was long with knots tied into the leather tails. She winced as he flicked the air, testing the whip with a resounding crack.

"Charles, you are charged with failure to obey a direct order from your master, Mica, as well as your king. Your negligence nearly cost the lives of two of our own. Your punishment is ten lashes. I will administer the first five and your master the last. Do you understand why you're being punished?"

Charles openly wept. "Yes, sire, I consider myself fortunate that you didn't kill me on the spot."

"Mark my words, if either of them had died, you would be dead now. And there are no second chances. If it happens again, you will not live long enough to see punishment."

153

Charles's head bobbed furiously. "Yes, sire, I understand."

Drake reared back his arm, letting the whip fly, the knotted ends landing on the poor man's back.

Charles cried out, arching his back away from the whip, as the knots tore into his bared flesh, streaking his back in crimson.

Sherry watched as the whip struck four more times before Drake handed it to Mica. She held her chin up and her gaze steady as Mica finished the deed. The same two vampires approached again and unchained the man, laying his unconscious body face down on the table. They forced him to wake as one of them applied salve to the open wounds; the other opened his vein and encouraged the injured man to drink. To those in attendance she appeared calm and in control, but all the while her stomach churned with revulsion as she watched in horror.

Drake sat next to her in his throne. *I am proud of you. You have held up well.*

She frowned. *You gave me no choice.*

He reached over and squeezed her stiff fingers. *For that I apologize, love. I couldn't tell you what was about to happen before we left our room. It was important that you were in attendance, and if I had told you ahead of time I don't think you would have left the room.*

Probably not.

Be proud. You have earned the respect of your subjects.

She glanced around the room before responding, swallowing back the bile in the back of her throat. *Fine, whatever, may I go back to our room now?*

Why, what's wrong?

Do you think I'd lose their respect if I puked my guts out in front of them?

He cut his eyes at her. *Fine, go back to our room, but try to be discreet about it. Lie down and try to get some rest. I have a few things to finish up here. Later tonight, at midnight to be exact, you will be coroneted as their queen.*

Are you trying to make me feel worse?

The corners of his mouth turned up in a smile. "Go lie down and get some rest, love."

She rolled her eyes and smiled back. "Thank you, sire."

Karen Fuller

Chapter Nineteen

She heaved a final time as her stomach protested to the little that remained. Her knees ached from kneeling in front of the toilet. She rose and wet a washcloth, running it over the back of her neck and across her face. If she never had to watch something like that again it would be too soon.

Closing the lid, she sat down on the toilet and breathed a sigh of relief. Her stomach had finally quieted. The cell phone in her back pocket vibrated. She fished it out and looked at the screen. It was a number she wasn't familiar with, leaving her to debate whether or not to even answer it. In the end she gave in and hit the talk button. "Hello?"

"I was beginning to wonder if you were going to answer the phone, bitch."

Sherry frowned and looked at the number on the LCD screen again. She didn't recognize the number or the voice. "I don't know who you are asshole, but I'm hanging up now."

"Hang up and the whelp dies, bitch."

A cold chill ran up her spine. *Mica*. She didn't see little Mica or Caleb in the throne room. "Who is this?"

"You don't worry about *who* this is. You just worry about keeping the whelp alive for a time."

"You harm a hair on his head and I'll—"

"You're in no position to threaten us, bitch. In fact, you couldn't hurt us if you tried. You'll do as you're told."

"What do you want?"

"For starters we want you to walk out on the dock behind the building, alone. If you alert the others he's a dead cat."

"You can't…he's just a boy."

"The clock is ticking, bitch."

"They'll never let me leave alone."

"For the whelp's sake you better be wrong about that. Tic tock tic tock—"

"No, please."

"You have five minutes." Then the connection cut.

***

Sherry opened the chamber door and peeked around the corner. The hallway was empty. She could hear the meeting still going on in the throne room, so for now the coast was clear. She made a run for it down the hallway toward the rear door into the alleyway. What she was doing petrified her, but she couldn't let them hurt little Mica. That boy was innocent and held a special place in her heart.

She opened the door and stepped out into the alleyway into the cool night air. The heavy door swung shut behind her with a resounding click. Out of the shadows five men appeared and surrounded her. Mica was nowhere to be seen. "What have you done with him?"

The leader stepped forward. He wore a sinister grin and he looked remarkably like a younger version of Caleb except for the cold glint in his eyes and the hard lines around his mouth. He looked to his friends and they all laughed, mocking her. "What've I done with whom?"

Her heart thudded in her chest. "The boy…where's Mica?"

"That's why we want you, bitch. We want to use you as leverage to get the whelp."

Fear clutched at her heart. She looked around at her surroundings in desperation and whispered, "By the power of three times three, let him see, let him see." Then she reached behind her for the doorknob and tried to twist it. Locked. "Shit!"

The leader grabbed her by the arm, twisting it behind her back. "Your spell didn't work, lady. I don't see anything I ain't supposta see. It looks like we've captured us a witch, boys." Their laughter rang out again and her heart turned cold. He twisted her arm higher and shoved her toward a car just under the street lamp. The engine revved and the lights came on, indicating that there was another person involved in this kidnapping.

"Ow! Watch it asshole, that hurts."

He shoved her into the backseat. "Get used to it sweet cheeks, we're just getting started."

Sherry slammed into the back of the front seat, jarring her shoulder, and found herself face to face with the driver, Justin Hargrove. He gave her a toothy grin. "Miss me, witch?"

If Sherry had anything left in her stomach she would have thrown up on the spot as the bile left the taste of fear in the back of her throat. "You're a dead man," she managed to croak.

He threw back his head and laughed. "I don't feel too dead. Actually I feel quite fine, very healthy in fact. Do I look dead to you boys?"

"Naw, Justin, you look like you always do. Alive and kickin'."

"What do you want with me?"

"We already told you, sweet cheeks. We're using you as bait to draw out the whelp. Our buddy, Justin here, well, he'll take over from there."

Sherry swallowed hard. "How did you even know about the boy?"

Their leader leered at her. "We had help from the inside, lady. It appears that not everyone is in love with their new queen."

***

Drake and Mica stood around a large table studying a map. Drake pointed to a desolate road. "Santana's clan should be coming in from this direction."

Mica shook his head. "No, that would be an obvious route. I don't think Santana is that stupid. He would assume that you would expect him to come from that direction. I think he'll come from here." Mica's finger traced a main road.

Desiree sat on a stool at the end of the table. "When are you expecting them to attack?"

Drake sighed and ran his fingers through his hair. "It could be anytime. The signs are right."

Desiree looked up from the map. "Signs?"

Drake nodded. "You know of the three sisters?"

Her eyes widened in surprise. "Are you referring to the Fates?"

"Yes."

"I didn't know you believed in that kind of stuff."

Mica looked between them. "What are you two talking about?"

Desiree leaned over the table on her elbows and clasped her hands in front of her. "The Fates, Mica, they're reputed to be three powerful witches, prophets really. Some say they're immortal. We've all grown up hearing the fables, but I've never seen anything to prove to me that they're actually real."

Drake crossed his arms over his chest, glaring at her. "They're real."

Desiree laughed. "What are you telling me, Drake? Are you saying that you've actually seen them?"

Drake nodded and the smile fell from Desiree's face. "They were responsible for my conversion, Mica's too for that matter."

Mica did a double take. "What?"

"They laid their hands on me and calmed my cravings. They told me to convert you, Mica, and build an army. It wasn't by accident that we won the vampire wars in England three hundred years ago."

Desiree threw up her hands to halt Drake's speech. "Okay, Drake, let's say that I believe you for argument's sake. That was three hundred years ago. What does all this have to do with the here and now?"

"The vampire wars were some of the bloodiest battles that I've ever seen." Mica nodded in agreement as Drake spoke. "We overthrew our opposition, practically annihilating them from the face of the planet."

Mica nodded again. "Yes, that's right. I remember."

"As my reward the sisters told me to set sail for America and to take Mica with me. They said to build an army. They told me that when I found my soul mate a new vampire war would begin. I was told to keep my loved ones close, and that there would be betrayal by someone close to me, to trust no one. If I were to win this war, I would rein for eternity as king." Desiree and Mica shared a glance as Drake continued. "When I heard about Santana vying for my kingdom I knew that I would soon find my soul mate and the war would begin again."

Desiree swallowed hard. "Drake, have you told any of this to Sherry?"

"Yes, all of it."

Desiree slapped her palm down on the table. "Dammit, Drake! If we lose this war then I lose my best friend, because if something happens to you then she dies too."

"We will not lose."

Mica looked up at Drake. "Their army is three times the size of ours."

"We. Will. Not. Lose." Drake shouted.

Desiree frowned at Mica. "You're right, Drake, we will not lose. Whether I like it or not you are the key to Sherry's survival. There is no walking away for either of us now. I guess the Fates really do exist. They have woven both Sherry and I so tightly into your world it is either fight or die with you." She slapped her palm on the table again with conviction. "Sherry and I will use our magic to fight beside you to help you win this war. Our combined magic will help even the odds a bit."

Caleb entered the room. "I'm in."

Mica glared at his friend. "Where have you been?"

Caleb shrugged. "I had to buy the boy some clothes."

Desiree slapped Caleb on the shoulder in irritation. "He's not 'the boy,' Caleb, he's your son."

"I know, I know, Dez. I'm still trying to get used to 'the dad' thing. He seems to be a pretty good kid."

"Yeah, because he wasn't raised around you...don't ruin him."

"Hey...."

Desiree narrowed her eyes to glower at the shifter. "I mean it, Caleb. He's a good kid. If I catch him acting like you then I'll be looking at you to blame."

"Admit it, Dez, you know you love me."

Desiree sighed heavily. "Mica, a little help here before I decide to throw another fireball at him."

"Caleb, we've been through this."

"Okay, Mica, I get it. You got the girl. I'll back off."

Drake shook his head. He never understood the friendship between Mica and Caleb, but as bad as he hated to admit it, he needed Caleb's help now. "I'm glad you're here, Caleb. We can use the help."

Caleb blinked, eyes wide. "I never thought I'd live to hear you say you were happy to see me, Drake." He patted his hands on his own chest. "Wait, I'm still alive aren't I?" He burst out laughing.

Drake frowned. "Don't get cocky about it."

Mica glared at Caleb. "Caleb! This is no time for horsing around. Things will be getting ugly very soon and we need everyone focused."

"I'm just trying to lighten the mood a bit."

Desiree rolled her eyes. "We make a very strange family."

Drake tilted his head. "Your meaning?"

She shrugged. "Three species that don't generally get along: witches, vampires and shape shifters. Brought together by fate, we are combining our forces for a common goal—to survive."

Karen Fuller

164

Chapter Twenty

Drake nodded at Desiree. "I agree. We are all stronger fighting together."

Desiree sat back on the stool. "Wow, I'm feeling a bit like Caleb now. You're actually agreeing with me."

Drake's gaze leveled with hers. "I'll go one better." Desiree sat up, listening intently. "Help me win this war and I will grant you your freedom."

Desiree reached for Mica's hand without taking her eyes from Drake's. "Swear it. Swear it to me now in front of these witnesses."

"I am a man of my word."

"When it suits you."

Drake's eyes flashed red as his jaw clenched in anger.

"Desiree!" Mica shook his head at her in warning.

She closed her eyes, and her shoulders sagged. "Fine, I'm sorry, Drake." She opened her eyes and leveled her gaze with Drake's. "That remark was uncalled for. It's just...you really upset me when you wouldn't release me."

Drake took a few calming breaths. "I know, but when I took you to begin with, I didn't know how powerful you really were. With the power in the amulets you convinced me that you might be the key to winning this coming war. I needed you as an ally, fighting on my side. I had no idea that

I would find my soul mate through you. I guess the Fates have a twisted sense of humor."

"If I felt the cause was right, I would have still fought by your side, without the bondage."

Mica nodded. "Same here."

In that moment Drake realized that his firstborn and his firstborn's mate were his true friends, not just subjects to order to do his bidding. He knew what he had to do. "I release you, Desiree Dupuis, from bondage. You are free. And you, Mica, you have always been my friend, even when I didn't deserve it. If the Fates hadn't intervened I don't know that I would have turned you, but you have been a powerful friend and ally these last three hundred years. I should have released you long ago. You were always an alpha like me and meant to have your own clan. I release...."

Drake froze, staring straight ahead. His hands gripped the sides of the table, the wood splintering beneath the pressure.

Caleb leaned forward and waved his hand in front of Drake's face, getting no response. "What's wrong with him?"

Desiree snapped her fingers in front of Drake's face a couple of times with the same results. "I'm not sure, but I believe that he's having a vision." She turned to her mate. "Mica, do vampires have visions?"

"Only when we're in tune with our mates."

"But Sherry's supposed to be in their chambers resting. Why would she be sending him a vision?"

Caleb smirked. "Maybe it's her way of summoning him to her bed."

Mica slapped Caleb on the backside of his head. "Get your mind out of the gutter. Our visions don't work like that fu—you almost had me calling you 'fur ball' with cracks like that."

Caleb smiled. "Ah, you just reminded me of Denise, I'm gonna have to look her up. I kinda miss her callin' me that."

Desiree frowned. "Caleb, focus." She turned to her mate. "Mica, how do your visions work?"

"When needed we can see through our mate's eyes. And from the look of that grip Drake has on the edge of the table, I'm assuming he's not too happy with what he's seeing."

Desiree hopped off the barstool. "Excuse me."

Mica sat back. "Where are you going?"

"To check on Sherry."

"The odds of her being in their chamber are nil. Somehow, someone has gotten to her."

"You better be wrong, because if you're not, we're all in trouble. Sherry is more powerful than even she knows. She just believes that she is a common witch. She doesn't know that she was born with natural powers. With the right training, she alone would be an unstoppable force. That is one of the reasons that I have kept such close tabs on her throughout the years. That, and I never told her, but she is my great-great-granddaughter."

Caleb slapped his forehead. "Wow, Dez, you never told us you had a kid."

"It was safer for all those concerned not to know. The witch hunters were always after me, and if they knew about my offspring they would be in danger too. Shortly after I cast that spell and realized that I no longer aged, my husband died in an accident. Caroline was only fifteen at the time. I arranged a marriage for her and told her that I had to disappear for a while to keep her safe. I was lucky because she happened to be in love with the boy to begin with. She agreed to keep my secret. I watched her from afar as she had children and grew old. When she was an old woman I came back. She introduced me to her children, my grandchildren, as a friend and a coven leader. I've stayed in touch with them all in that capacity ever since."

Mica took her hand in his and kissed it. "Now I understand why you were so protective of the girl."

"Since her mother died, she is the last of my line."

"We will get her back, love."

"We better get her back. I not only love her, but that kind of power in the wrong hands can be deadly."

"What do you mean?"

"I mean that if Sherry and I combine our powers together we are strong enough to stop this war before it ever begins."

Mica lifted an eyebrow. "That's impossible, love…the enemy is over three thousand strong."

She nodded. "It's a drop in the bucket for what we'd be capable of together."

Caleb let out a long low whistle. "I've seen what you can do alone…."

Desiree gave Drake a worried look in his frozen state. "We better pray that they don't discover what they have."

Drake blinked a couple of times and began to shake in a deep rage as he came out of the trance. The color of his eyes change to blood red, his upper fangs elongated over his bottom lip, the tendons in his neck bulged under the pressure, and then the edge of the table beneath his fingers suddenly shattered. He stood, then raised his fist in the air and slammed it on the tabletop, causing it to shatter in pieces on the floor. "I will rip the head off that snake with my teeth and feed it to the alligators in the bayou. Then I will eat his heart," he roared.

Chapter Twenty-One

Desiree's face paled. "Who has my baby, Drake?"

In Drake's state of mind he was feral, seeing the entire room in an angry shade of red. He had heard Desiree's explanation in his frozen state, but had been unable to respond to it until now. He backed against the wall in an effort to control his rage. "Our baby has been kidnapped by more than one." His voice was horse and strained. "Justin Hargrove seems to be the one in control."

Desiree brought her hands up over her mouth in horror. "He'll kill her. She doesn't even know she has the power within her to defeat him."

"There are others." He turned and cast his gaze on Caleb. "There is one who looks remarkably like you." He pointed a clawed finger in Caleb's direction. "He wants the boy."

"He can't have him." Caleb shook his fists in anger. His eyes shifted to panther and his voice changed to the scream of a large cat as his body rippled and black fur covered his hands. *"I will destroy them!"*

A glass shattered as it hit the ground. Little Mica stood in the doorway. His eyes bugged in shock as he glanced frantically around the room. "Where's Aunt Sher?"

Tears spilled from Desiree's eyes as she shook her head at the boy, unable to speak.

"*NO,*" he screamed. His head whipped back in forth in denial. "No, no, no, no! They have taken everything from me. They can't have her too!" Before their eyes the boy's new cloths ripped as he morphed into a white tiger twice the size and muscle mass of his father. He let out a fierce scream that had them all cover their ears.

Mica slapped Caleb on the back. "He's an alpha."

Caleb, still in mid-change, smiled. His long fangs protruded below his chin. "Yes, it appears so."

Desiree stepped around Mica to approach the boy. She reached out and stroked his fur. "This is why they wanted him. He is magnificent. They somehow knew what he would become. They either want to destroy him or train him to be their leader."

Caleb narrowed his glowing green eyes. "With their hatred of me, I am assuming that they were looking to destroy him."

The boy ran his rough tongue up the side of Desiree's face. She smiled sadly and wrapped her arms around his neck in a hug. "You will help to save her."

Caleb charged forward. "*NO.*"

"It is the only way." She looked to Drake. "They won't know what hit them."

***

Justin Hargrove put the car in gear, then looked into the rearview mirror. "Cedric, you and your boys need to tie her up tight. Don't want to give her a chance to cast a spell."

Cedric laughed. "She's already tried that on me, Justin. She failed miserably."

Justin looked up sharply into the rearview mirror. "What exactly did she say?"

He shrugged. "Something about multiplying and seeing. I didn't see nothing out of the ordinary."

"You're a fool! She didn't mean for *you* to see, stupid."

Cedric growled low and drew a claw down the side of Justin's neck, leaving a welt of blood in its wake. "Care to repeat yourself human?"

Justin swallowed hard. "No. I've dealt with witches before. If she says something that sounds strange it usually means something, that's all."

"I think you're wrong, witchy man."

"Fine, believe what you want."

"Just drive, witchy man and leave the witch to me." Cedric sat back and leisurely ran his claw down the side of Sherry's breast, slicing the fabric, exposing a little of her pale skin.

Her fingers pulled at her bindings behind her back as she tried to jerk away from his touch. "Keep your filthy paws off me."

He grabbed her breast, wrenching it painfully, bringing tears to her eyes. "You don't give me orders, witch." He then grabbed her hair by the nape of her neck, pulling her head back as he shoved his other hand painfully between her legs. "I will touch any part of you I wish to touch, and there ain't a damn thing you can do about it."

She squealed in protest and fought with everything she had. "I will enjoy watching Drake rip your fucking heart out!"

His eyes blazed with an unnatural glow as he reared his fist and punched her in the stomach. "Shut up, bitch!" He brought his fist up again.

Cedric's friend caught his wrist before he could deliver another blow and tugged him away. "Hey, Ced, she's right man. That vamp's a big dude. He'll kill you if he finds out that you've messed with his woman. Besides, he has a thousand vampires at his disposal to hunt us down. She ain't worth it man. Stay focused on our goal."

Sherry coughed and heaved, gasping for breath as the pain consumed her. Her shoulders and arms also burned from the tight position they had her hands tied from behind. She silently wished she hadn't been sick earlier so she could puke on him now. She squeezed her eyes shut, swallowing back the bile burning her throat.

Cedric grabbed a handful of hair and yanked her head up. "Stay with us, sweet cheeks." Her eyes opened, then narrowed as she clenched her jaw and scowled. He flashed her a smile. "Still feisty, I see. I'm sure your spirit will break when you see your little kitten fall beneath the master. You don't want to miss the show now, do you? We're here."

Jason put the car in park and cut the engine.

"I will kill you if it is the last thing I do."

He tilted his head. "Ah, but there in lies the kicker, sweet cheeks. You are only here as the bait. Once I devour your precious little kitten, Justin here has his own plans for you. I get to kill the boy and take pleasure in watching the anguish and grief consume that sorry father of ours, and Justin here…I'm not really sure what he has planned for you, but I rather doubt you'll live long enough to attempt to kill me."

Her mouth gaped. "Our father?"

"You look all too surprised to find out that that little whelp's father is my father too."

"I've only met Caleb once. He was surprised to find out Mica was his child. He said he didn't have any others."

"That fucking asshole didn't stick around long enough after fucking my mother to find out, now did he?"

"I've heard the story. Your pack nearly killed him for what he did to your mother."

"They would've finished the job, too, if that vamp hadn't shown up and killed my mother's husband, the pack's alpha. After I was born my mother saw the resemblance to my true father and knew her dead mate hadn't sired me. She cast me out of her home, cursing me as a bastard child. She said looking at me made her feel dirty and that I came from a bad seed. I was just a child and my own mother hated me because I looked like my father. I was forced to live on the dirty streets and beg for whatever scraps anyone would toss an outcast.

"I showed her though. I grew up strong, despite her best efforts, and I formed my own pack. *I* am the alpha now, and *I* didn't deem *her* fit to call *her* my mother. She begged for death by the time I was through with her. Now I'm moving on to the next ungrateful family member."

"Mica's not responsible for anything Caleb did. He's just a child. He's your brother."

"Yeah, a little snot nosed kid that got everything that was denied to *me*. I took great pleasure in making sure he didn't have a mother's love either. Oh, and she begged for her life and his too. That bitch gave *him* everything my mother refused to give me—a mother's love, plenty to eat, and a decent home. I couldn't let her or the little brat live. It wasn't fair to *me*. *I* was the firstborn. *I* deserved a better life more than he did. He was nothing but a traitor's leftovers. What made him think he deserved a better life than me? I am an alpha. I am a king!

"I knew what I had to do and the deed wasn't hard either. It just took one swipe of these babies." He wiggled his fingers in front of her face. "She died a little too easy. I wanted to make her suffer like I'd suffered over the years, but she just died. My own mama was harder to kill than that, I guess because she was a shifter too. I don't know, but I struck that bitch again because it pissed me off when I realized I killed her before she gave him up. I figured he'd be hiding, so I set fire to the place. I had assumed he died when a little birdie whispered in my ear, telling me that he still lived. It's taken me until now to find the little monster."

"He's a sweet kid. He didn't deserve what you did to him."

Cedric gripped her hair again, shoving her forward out of the car. "And you think I deserved what was done to me, bitch?"

"No, of course not. No child deserves that. Your mother should have been horsewhipped."

"Yeah, yeah, says you," he said as he shoved her forward again.

Sherry stumbled, hitting her shoulder on a leaning light pole. "Shit!" She leaned heavily against the pole to regain her footing.

Cedric pushed her again. "Stop stallin' bitch."

Sherry trudged forward as she looked around. The other shifters flanked her on each side. Justin walked ahead in the lead. The cold February wind blew into the rip in her shirt, sending gooseflesh across her body.

She had grown up in New Orleans and knew exactly where she was. They had brought her to the abandoned Six Flags theme park. The Katrina ravaged theme park was a testament to the horrors the city suffered in 2005. Debris littered the crumbling parking lot. The rollercoaster stood eerily in the distance, hauntingly still in its silence. Other rides were a mangled mess of broken parts and rust. Graffiti added to the desolation.

It had to be close to midnight. She should have been attending her coronation and embracing her new life, not leading that sweet boy into an ambush. Her heart ached. She could very well be responsible for getting them all killed.

Drake, I'm sorry. I never really told you that I loved you, but I do, she thought.

I love you too, vixen.

She caught her breath in surprise. *Drake?*

We're not far behind you, love.

Her heart raced. *No, don't come, it's a trap.*

I know. Your spell worked. I saw what happened.

She looked over her shoulder and Cedric shoved her forward again.

"Keep movin', bitch."

You have to make sure little Mica stays behind. They'll kill him.

He insisted on coming, love.

No, please. I couldn't bear it if something happened to him. I love that kid, Drake.

I know you do, but trust me, that kid has a big surprise in store for those men. He's a brave kid and he'll be okay, you'll see.

Drake, there's something you need to know. Their leader, Cedric, he's Caleb's son.

What?

I thought you saw everything.

I was able to see up to the point of the car speeding away...I thought that bastard looked remarkably like Caleb.

That story Mica told about Caleb and his pack—Caleb got that woman pregnant. She shunned the child and this is what we ended up with—a cold-blooded killer.

How did he get mixed up with the witch hunter?

I don't know, but when I asked him how he found out about Mica he said that not everyone is happy that I'm the new queen, and a little birdie from your group gave him the information.

We have a traitor.

Do you have any idea who it is?

No, but the Fates said there would be a traitor and to trust no one.

Be careful, Drake.

You too, love. Just keep cooperating until I get there. I can sense your general direction. It would help speed things up if you can tell me exactly where you are.

We're at the abandoned Six Flags theme park.

***

Justin led their group to the center of the theme park where the different sections split off to go to the different main attractions. He grabbed Sherry's arm. "You'll have your standoff here, boys. By now I'm sure they're on their way to rescue our little queen here."

Cedric placed his hands on his hips, glaring at Justin. "Doesn't someone need to make a phone call or somethin' first?"

Justin shook his head. "No need, boys. She's been in contact with them from the beginning."

Cedric scratched his head. "Come again?"

"It was a small matter of that little spell you said for me not to worry about because it didn't work. She's led them here to us—to you."

"You lyin' sack of shit."

Justin shoved Sherry forward. "Tell them *Queen* Sherry." She turned her head and glared back at Justin. He pushed her again. "*Tell them.*"

Cedric crossed his arms over his chest. "Yes, *Queenie*, spill it."

She glared at them all, then raised her chin in the direction they came from. "There's no use in lying to you because they're already here." The sound of screeching tires sounded in the distance, indicating their arrival.

Cedric threw back his head and laughed, then clapped his hands together, rubbing them briskly in anticipation. "Excellent!"

Justin yanked Sherry back again. "You have what you want. I'm taking the girl to fulfill my end."

Cedric leveled his gaze with Justin. "Just so you know, if you've double crossed me, I'll hunt you down and feast on your heart."

Jason smiled, holding his hand up in salute. "Have a nice life. I'll be able to retire after this transaction." He yanked on her arm, dragging her to the back of the park by the rollercoaster.

"Where are you taking me?"

"To your destiny. You see, Cedric isn't the only one with an agenda. The money I'll get from handing you over will set me and my daddy up for life."

She felt the laugh tickle the back of her throat as she tried unsuccessfully to hold it back. It erupted into a loud heartfelt belly laugh. Tears of mirth streamed down her face and she had to stop walking to catch her breath.

Justin stopped and turned to her, and his expression had her laughing harder. "I find it strange for a woman to laugh when the people I turn her over to are probably going to kill her."

"They may try," she choked out between bouts of laughter.

Justin placed his hands on his hips. "And you find that funny?"

She shook her head, laughing harder. "No, it's just...hahaha."

"It's just what?" he spat impatiently.

"Hahaha…I just had a visual of what you said…hahahaha…You living it up with your daddy…hahaha, that was just too funny."

"And how is my daddy and I living it up in the lap of luxury funny to you? You will probably be dead, and I would think that you should find that distressing, not funny."

"Have you seen your daddy lately, Justin? Hehehe."

"No, not in about a week." He replied honestly. "He'll turn up. He always does. He's probably tracking your friend again."

"Hehe…he tracked my friend one too many times. She finally got tired of it and dealt with the problem."

Justin frowned. "What do you mean by that?"

"Your daddy's been a guest at the warehouse for the last two days, dummy."

"You're lying. My daddy wouldn't stay voluntarily with a bunch of bloodsuckers."

She stopped laughing and flashed him a smile. "Did I say guest? I'm sorry, I misspoke. His accommodations are a gilded cage of sorts. Your daddy is a hairy rat."

"Now I know you're lying, bitch."

She looked up in the air as she thought. "We'll just see who's lying. Now how did that spell Desiree recited go again? Oh yeah, I remember now." Her eyes narrowed and glared into his. "Come to me, spirit from the black of night. I call to thee with all my might. Curse this mortal who cowers before me. Curse him now so all might see. In his heart, he is a rat. Change his form to reflect that. Take him down to this concrete floor. Shrink him down forever more. Please grant this spell I ask of thee. I do so wish it. So mote it be!"

Justin screamed, and to her surprise he shrunk down into a rat. She hadn't really expected the spell to work. Instead, she had really expected him to laugh at her and take her captive again. She breathed in deeply and felt the surge of power flow through her. *Hummm,* she thought. She lifted her chin and yelled, "Fire!" The ropes binding her wrists burst into flames, falling away. She stretched the kinks out of her arms and shoulders, then ran back in the direction she had just come from.

***

Drake, Mica, Desiree, Caleb and little Mica climbed out of the Hummer. Desiree placed her hands on the boy's shoulders. "Mica, are you sure you're up to this?"

"Yes, ma'am. He killed my mama and now he has Aunt Sher. I can't allow him to kill her too."

She squeezed his shoulders and kissed him on the cheek. "We'll be right behind you, son. Save her for me."

The boy smiled. "I will."

Desiree smiled back. "May the gods smile on you tonight." She turned to face the others. "Sherry's strong. I know she's alright. She won't be cowering in a corner like a little lost child. She'll find the power within herself and help us defeat them. Now, let's stop this reign of terror so that we can all get back to our lives."

Desiree looked up at the sky churning above their heads and lightning flashed, causing her to smile. "There is some powerful magic brewing tonight. Let's go."

The five strode across the parking lot and through the gate. Once past the gate the park was dark. The smell of mildew was strong in the air. Rusted metal creaked and groaned in the brisk breeze. Long shadows were cast behind them like growing giants in the light of the full moon.

Drake pointed to the left. "Mica you take the left." He turned, pointing in the other direction. "Caleb, you take the right. I'll stay in the middle with Desiree and the boy to directly face the kidnappers."

179

Caleb looked between Mica and Drake as if undecided before he spoke. "Drake, shouldn't I be the one in the middle, since it's my kids involved?"

Drake frowned. "No, Caleb. You need to stay out of sight as much as possible. If he sees you he may become unstable. He's already a ticking bomb as it is. I'm sorry, but we need no misunderstandings. Your son, Cedric, will not survive this night. He can't be allowed to live."

Caleb nodded. "I understand."

Drake lifted an eyebrow. "Do you?"

"Yes."

"Have you ever lost a child before?"

Caleb shook his head. "No, but—"

"It will tear up your insides."

"Drake, you really don't know me. I think—"

"I lost the only child I will ever have three hundred years ago. My unborn son died in childbirth along with my wife. I know what you will feel to lose a child. Even though you've never met the child, he's still a part of you. You will see yourself in him. Do not let this cloud your judgment."

Caleb exchanged a look with Mica. "He's right, Caleb, you need to stay hidden until it's time."

"Fine, agreed."

"Come out, come out, wherever you are," echoed throughout the empty park.

Desiree ran her hand over the boy's shoulders. "It appears we've lost the element of surprise."

Drake's jaw clenched. "We will win this night."

"Agreed," the others responded.

The boy splayed his hands. "What are we waiting for? Let's go get Aunt Sher."

Drake ruffled the boy's hair, then clapped him on the back. "I agree. Let's go."

The three made their way through the road in the center while Mica and Caleb skirted the buildings on opposite sides to stay hidden. The boy was in the center leading the way when they stepped out into the open hub of the park.

Drake noted Cedric leisurely sitting on top of a low building with his arm draped casually across a knee. He watched him stand and jump down as they approached the center. He scanned the area. The others remained hidden.

Drake crossed his arms over his broad chest. "You have my mate. Where is she?"

A cocky smile played across Cedric's face, and he shrugged, splaying his hands. "Do you *see* your mate anywhere, sire?" He threw back his head and laughed. "More than likely she's meeting her end as we speak."

"No!" the boy cried out and took a forward step. Drake placed a staying hand on his shoulder.

"Not yet," he spoke in a low tone to the boy. He spoke louder. "You do realize that you've signed your own death warrant. None of you are going to make it out of here alive."

The smile left Cedric's face. "It is you and your group who will not live." He pointed an accusing finger at the boy. "I've hunted for him long enough. I will get my revenge. He will die tonight as will you all."

The boy clenched his fists at his sides. "What did I ever do to you?"

Cedric looked bored as he replied, "You took your first breath."

"What?"

"You live, boy, isn't that enough?"

"You hate me because I was born? *You* murdered my mother because she gave birth to me?"

Cedric tilted his head. "Essentially, yes."

***

Drake, I'm here.

Drake looked up and saw Sherry standing on top of the building Cedric had just vacated. He nodded slightly. *It's good to see you, vixen.*

She smiled broadly. *It's good to be seen again.*

Hargrove?

Her smile grew. *He's met the same fate as his father.*

Drake nudged Desiree. When she glanced his way he indicated with his eyes to look on top of the building.

She kept the smile from her face and said "good" under her breath.

Let's finish this, vixen.

She jumped down from the building. *Gladly.*

***

The four shifters appeared from the shadows to flank their leader.

The boy raised his chin a notch. "You've taken everything from me for no reason at all."

"You are *his* son. That's reason enough."

"You are too."

Cedric's eyes widened. "You know who I am?"

"Sure. You're my brother, and a psychotic son of a bitch with no redeeming qualities. I feel cursed to even be related to you."

Caleb stepped out of the shadows to stand behind the boy. He placed his hands on the boy's shoulders to stand united.

Cedric scowled, pointing an accusing finger at Caleb. "So, the mighty Caleb Jenkins finally makes an appearance, the ever elusive father. Hello, Father, it took you long enough. I've hunted you for the last two hundred and fifty years."

"Then you suck as a tracker, because I've been right here in New Orleans. I've never felt a need to hide."

Cedric's scowl deepened at the insult, then he grinned evilly. "Ever wonder why a lot of your ladies just disappeared and never called you back?" Caleb narrowed his eyes. "I see we understand each other. I was making sure you didn't populate the earth." His grin broadened when he saw his father scowl. "But for some reason that bitch Celia slipped my notice. Maybe it was because you didn't pick her up randomly in some bar like you did the rest. Imagine my surprise when I discovered *he* existed."

"I loved Celia."

"I *know*, that's why she had to die."

"Because I loved her?"

"Yes, I want to see you suffer before I eat your heart."

Cedric felt a tap on his shoulder and turned his head. Sherry flashed him a hateful smile. "Miss me?"

His eyes widened. "How?"

She balled up her fist, clocking him on the jaw.

Cedric stumbled with the unexpected blow. Rage rippled through him as his body phased into a large black panther. He let out an ear-piercing scream of rage as he reared up his large paw to strike.

The other shifters phased and flanked their leader.

"No!" young Mica screamed as he charged forward. In a single step he phased into the white tiger.

"Another outfit," Caleb mumbled in disgust as he stripped his own clothes off. "The kid's gonna break my bank account buying him clothes."

Desiree smacked his arm. "Shut up, Caleb!"

The white tiger pounced on Cedric before he could strike Sherry. They rolled on the ground with claws and teeth tearing into each other. They were evenly matched. Mica was larger and stronger, but Cedric had more experience and fought dirty.

Drake and Mica rushed forward to take on the other shifters. Caleb shifted into a panther, jumping in the middle of the fight.

Desiree ran up to Sherry, embracing her in a hug. "I was so afraid that I'd lost you."

Sherry shook her head and smiled. "I'm tougher than that."

"More than you know."

The battle raged around the women as teeth flashed and fur flew.

Young Mica rolled Cedric on his back. His mighty paws weighing down Cedric's heaving chest. Both were bloodied and exhausted. Caleb let out a mighty roar as he gazed at his young son. Cedric, sensing the end was near, struggled to regain his footing. Mica pounced on his chest again, then sank his teeth deep into Cedric's jugular. The enormous cat ceased his struggles, laying still in death.

The young cat stepped off his prey and started licking his wounds. His father stood beside him and ran his rough tongue over a bad gash in Mica's side.

Two of the cats lay dead and bleeding not far from their leader. Drake and Mica still fought the remaining two.

Sherry looked over her shoulder and caught her breath. She nudged Desiree to look away from the fight and whispered. "Oh god, we're surrounded."

Chapter Twenty-Two

Desiree looked up sharply to witness what Sherry was saying. They were indeed surrounded by about three thousand blood-thirsty vampires. "Oh, no. Santana's making his move, and Drake's here without his clan for support."

"Justin Hargrove planned this," Sherry whispered fiercely. "I just didn't know what he was talking about."

The circle slowly started to close in on their small group. Drake and Mica still fought the two remaining cats.

Desiree looked at Sherry. She saw the fear in the young woman's eyes. "Listen to me and listen closely. I don't have time to go into great detail but know this…you are not a common witch. You carry my powers." Sherry's eyes widened in surprise. "We will live to discuss this in length, but for now I need you to listen." Sherry nodded. "Do you remember the spell I told you that I cast on that clan of vampires a few days ago?"

"Yes, why?"

"We are stronger together. Our magic is stronger together. We can destroy them together."

"How?"

"Recite the spell with me. Together it will be strong enough to destroy them instead of just frighten them."

"But what about Drake and Mica?"

185

"They're protected by the amulets. Our spell will not harm them."

"We're running out of time. Let's try it. Anything's better than standing here and dying."

"Agreed."

They held hands, raised their fists in the air and began to chant:

"By the gods we beckon thee, to bring the sun so they will see. With its rays they doth feel, the kiss of fire to feel so real. To burn their flesh and cause them pain, to dissolve their bodies to where only ash remain. In this night and in this hour we call upon the ancient power. By the power of three times three, let them see, let them see. We do so wish it, so mote it be!"

Chaos suddenly sprouted everywhere as lightening streaked the sky and the clouds boiled and churned like an angry sea. The wind whipped up, blowing Desiree's and Sherry's hair and clothes furiously about them. Their bodies glowed and levitated into the air as the power surged around and through them.

Mica and Drake had just destroyed the two remaining cats, and stood in awe as their mates rose higher into the air. It was then they became aware that the cats weren't their only opponents. The real enemies were there, now, and they were sorely outnumbered. There was no time to call in their clan.

Drake's jaw clenched in anger as he watched Santana strut proudly to the front of his group.

Santana smiled triumphantly and gestured to the women in the air. "Nice show, Drake, but it will take more than parlor tricks to defeat me. Your kingdom is mine. You no longer rule here. Two lone vampires and a couple of shape shifters can't defeat my army. Face it Drake, you're done."

Caleb and young Mica flanked their friends. Drake nodded to them, then glared at Santana. "Fuck you, Santana."

Santana wagged his finger in the air. "You are in no position for name calling."

"I will die before submitting my kingdom to you."

"That was always the plan from the beginning. Never leave your enemy alive to strike back."

"I am not afraid to die, Santana."

"I never took you for a coward, Drake. On the contrary, you've always been a strong and respected leader. You're just in the way of what I want—this great city."

"You can't have it."

Santana laughed. "I somehow knew you wouldn't want to give up without a fight."

The ground trembled beneath their feet as the two witches floated back to the ground. The witches' eyes glowed blue and they appeared to be in a deep trance.

The women turned and stepped apart, but stayed back to back and raised their hands stretched out level with their chests. Blue rays emitted from their fingers out into the throng of vampires. Everyone the rays touched burst into flames, dissolving into ash.

Another type of chaos arose as the vampires pushed and shoved each other to get out of the way of the unnatural light. Screams of pain and anguish rent the air as the wounded fell and died.

Santana roared in anger. "What in the hell is going on?" He ducked around a beam of light and made a wide berth around the group.

Amidst the ruckus and confusion Santana managed to slip in between the women. He drew his dagger and shoved it into Sherry's back. She fell in a heap onto the concrete. Her blood rushed and pooled around her body.

Santana roared in triumph. "I will still win this night."

Drake rushed his enemy. "Not if I can help it." He tackled Santana to the ground. They wrestled and rolled, with knives and teeth.

Desiree came out of her trance, screaming as she rushed to Sherry's side. "Drake, she's dying."

"Good," Santana grunted at the news as they continued to wrestle.

Drake straddled his opponent. "I'll see you in hell, Santana," He raised his dagger, plunging it into Santana's heart. Santana's hands dropped away as he lay frozen and unable to respond. Drake stood. "Mica, tie him up before you remove the dagger. He will stand trial." He made his way to Sherry and knelt next to Desiree. "Can't you cast a spell to heal her?"

Desiree's shoulders shook in anguish. "She's already lost too much blood for magic. He must have severed a main artery. She's dying, Drake, and I can't do a damn thing to stop it."

Sherry's eyes fluttered and her hand flopped away from her body. *Remember that I've always loved you.*

Hold on, love. Drake bit into his wrist and nudged Desiree out of the way. "I have no choice."

Desiree grabbed his arm. "No, Drake, she doesn't want to be a vampire."

Drake yanked his arm out of her grasp. "There's no other choice. Her heart is growing weaker. It's now or never...Mica! Come tend to your mate."

Desiree rushed into Mica's arms and wept.

Drake tilted Sherry's head back and let the blood from his wrist trickle into her mouth. It filled and spilled out of the sides. "Drink!" In frustration he pinched her nose and pressed his wrist firmly to her mouth. "Drink, damn it."

She choked, swallowed, then swallowed again. Her hands reached up, grabbing his arm, drinking now in earnest.

He stroked her hair. "You will live, little one. Your life will be different, but you'll remain by my side for eternity. Rest, love."

He pulled his hand back and sealed the wound with his saliva. He gathered Sherry into his arms, cradling her to his chest. "Desiree, will she keep her powers?"

Desiree shrugged, wiping the tears from her cheeks. "I honestly don't know. I've never heard of this happening to one of us before."

Chapter Twenty-Three

Sherry slowly opened her eyes. It was dark, but she saw everything clearly, down to the tiny minute cracks in the ceiling tiles. She cut her eyes to the right then to the left. She realized that she was in her bed at the warehouse. The memory of how she got there eluded her.

She retraced the steps in her mind; the kidnapping, changing Justin into a rat, the fight with the cats, and finally Santana's warriors. She sat up abruptly. *Santana's warriors! Drake's in trouble,* she thought. She moved and stood by the bed so fast her head swam. Pressing her palms against her eyes she cried out. "Drake!"

She heard the door open, then close. The sounds echoed in her head. Then she felt Drake wrap his arms around her, holding her close. *I'm here,* he spoke to her mind.

She turned into his arms and buried her face in his neck. "What's wrong with me?" She moved her hands to cover her ears. "Ah! Why is my voice so loud?"

He rubbed her back in a soothing manner, rocking her gently. *You were mortally wounded in the battle.*

Her voice caught. "What are you saying?"

I had to convert you, love.

"You mean I died?"

191

No, let's just say you were born again. You will never die, love.

"I thought you said I wouldn't become a vampire like you."

That wasn't my intention, no, but I guess that is what the Fates had planned all along. I knew that you would become immortal, but at the time I didn't know how. Had I been given a choice I would have tried to find another way, but Desiree said you were injured too badly for even magic to heal you. There wasn't time to find other help. Had I tried you would have been dead.

"Then you would have died too."

Yes.

"Why aren't you speaking out loud?"

He chuckled softly. *I could, but your senses will be in overdrive for the next couple of hours. You'll need to sit quietly for a few more hours until you feel a little more normal.*

She sighed heavily and snuggled a little deeper into his neck. "Okay. Mmmm you smell good."

Are you hungry?

"I'm starving."

You can feed from me. In fact, you need to feed.

"How?"

Run your tongue along the vein in my neck. Yes, that's right. You'll feel your teeth drop.

All her senses were heightened. He smelled so good her mouth watered. She ran her tongue along his neck, following the artery from the crook of his neck to his ear. She felt the familiar ache in her core as she ran her tongue over her teeth and felt their newfound sharpness. She bit down, sinking her teeth into the tender flesh of his neck, his blood flowing freely into her mouth.

He held her close, allowing her free reign to take what she needed from him.

She pulled her teeth back and sealed the wound with her tongue. "I'm still hungry."

You didn't have to stop.

"No." She fisted his shirt in her hands and flung him back on the bed with her new strength. "I need to feel you between my legs." She worked the button on her jeans, unzipped the zipper, and shimmied them to the floor. "I need to feel you deep inside me…." She pulled her sweater over her head and threw it to the floor. "To touch my soul." She stopped and raised an eyebrow. "You're still dressed?"

A smile touched his lips as he reached for the snap on his leather pants. "I figured that you'd be angry with me for changing you." The pants slid past his hips exposing his hard cock, then he kicked them the rest of the way off.

Sherry straddled his legs and sat down, considering his words. "I can't find it in myself to be angry with you. Would I have chosen this for myself? I would have to say no, but I do choose you, love. If it means living for eternity as a vampire to remain with you…well, I can't be angry with you about that."

His smile grew. "Good." Grabbing her hips he flipped her over on her belly, spreading her legs, exposing her fully to his gaze. On his knees now he peeled the shirt over his head. It followed the rest of the clothes to the floor. "Because I want to show you how it feels to feed from each other. But first…."

With one hand he fisted his cock, and with the other he pumped a finger in the slick opening, spreading her juices around and over her tight ass. Her inner walls clenched and wept.

Looking over her shoulder she asked, "What are you doing?"

"Relax, love. I'm going to heighten your pleasure. For now I'm only using my fingers." Dipping his fingers into her creamy wetness, he again used the wetness to massage the tiny bud, then slipped a finger into the opening.

Sherry moaned and undulated her hips to get closer to his hand. Plunging his finger slowly in and out, going deeper with each stroke, he eased his cock in past the silken lips and began to rock his hips in rhythm with his finger, pulling both nearly out to ram all the way back in, picking up the speed and abandon. Sherry threw back her head and bucked her hips, taking him in to the hilt. Her body shuddered over his cock and finger, pulsating and milking the swollen member.

Drake shoved his cock in as deep as it would go and roared out his own release. Removing his finger and cock, he rolled her over and buried his cock again in her wetness, undulating his hips to stoke her need again. Her inner wall still pulsated, sucking him deeper. He licked the vein in her neck. "Here's how we'll feed, love." He sank his fangs into the tender vein as his cock plunged deeper.

Sherry's body was on fire. Every movement of his hips wound her tighter than before, and the feel of his mouth on her neck was heaven. On the verge of her own climax, she sank her teeth into his shoulder. Together they crested and felt their souls merge as one.

***

Sherry dressed in a red velvet gown that Drake insisted that she wear. He had told her that she would receive her coronation, and there would also be a trial of sorts for Santana. They all already knew he was guilty…it was just a formality.

She brushed her hair as she looked into the mirror. Her eyes were now a deep shade of red. Drake had told her that her eyes would remain that color for about a year, then they would slowly change back to her natural color, and then only change if she were angry or on the hunt. Her complexion now was the color of flawless porcelain. She turned her face from side to side as she studied every detail. Being a vampire seemed to enhance the good parts of her features and hide the bad.

There were still a couple of unknowns: Was she still a witch? Could her body handle the sunlight without an amulet? She was anxious to find out.

Drake walked up behind her and placed his hands on her shoulders. He kissed her neck. "Are you ready, my queen?"

She placed the hairbrush on the counter and smiled at their reflection into the mirror. "Yes, sire."

He turned her around and kissed her lips gently, then placed her hand on the crook of his arm. "Let's go make this official."

This trip down the hall was different from the last. This time there were no secrets. They walked through the throne room doors arm in arm.

The entire clan stood at attention. They raised their right fists in the air, then across their hearts, and back in the air as a silent salute to their king and queen.

"My love, I need you to face the throne and kneel."

She gave him a half smile and kneeled as he asked.

Drake held her crown in his hands and held it up for all to see. "I have claimed my life mate and your new queen. Serve her as you would serve me." He placed the crown on her head. "Rise, my queen, and meet your subjects."

She rose, placed her hand on his arm again, then faced the clan. The entire clan saluted her with their fists. Drake led her to her throne and encouraged her to sit. He sat in his own throne and raised his hand for the meeting to continue.

"You did beautifully, vixen."

"Thank you." She looked around. "What's next?"

"We will hear and judge Santana together. Are you up to it?"

"The man almost succeeded in killing me. I will take great pleasure in sitting in judgment."

"Now vixen, we have to go by facts, not personal vendettas. We are supposed to be unbiased. Don't let the power go to your head."

"I count myself blessed to still be here. I won't be biased."

He nodded. "Good."

Drake lifted his hand and motioned with his fingers to bring the prisoner forward.

Santana swaggered to his place in front of the throne, his hands tied securely behind his back, chin held high.

Drake raised his hand for silence. "Santana, you are charged with plotting to overthrow my kingdom and attempting to kill my mate. How do you plead?"

"This kingdom should have been mine. It was promised to me. Your mate was in my way and just a means to an end. She should have died, thus ending you."

"Who promised you my kingdom? Was it the Fates?"

"Who?"

"Did the Fates promise you my kingdom?"

"No."

He's hiding something, Drake said to Sherry.

I think so too.

"Who promised you my kingdom?"

"It doesn't suit me to tell you."

"You are going to die, Santana. Would you rather die alone with your secret?"

"The deal is off, Sean."

Sean backed up toward the door.

Drake tilted his head and glared at his long-time servant. "Sean?"

Two guards stopped Sean by gripping his arms. "He lies, sire."

"A dead man has no need to lie. Why?"

"I was promised your throne."

Drake raised an eyebrow. "Do you honestly believe that Santana would have let you live long enough to rule? If you did, you are a bigger fool then you appear to be. Santana wanted to rule New Orleans himself. He told me so as he tried to kill me. The key focus is the word tried. Sean, you do not have the backbone to be a ruler. The others would not have followed you. If you had succeeded in getting me killed, another stronger vampire would have risen up and overthrown you. You don't have what it takes to be king."

Drake stood. "You both are sentenced to death." Drake looked to the guard. "Strip Sean of his amulet." The guard reached over and yanked the chain from his neck. "Take them to the plantation. It is secluded. Stake them outside. They will meet their end by meeting the sun."

Sean tried to yank away from the guard. "You can't do this! I demand to be set free."

Drake glared into his eyes. "You are in no position to make demands, Sean. You betrayed your own friends and sealed your own fate. Guards, take them away."

***

"I asked Mica and Desiree to meet us in our chambers."

"Why? What's going on?"

"I have to decide what to do with Santana's kingdom."

"You're not thinking of moving to Texas, are you?"

He chuckled softly. "No, love, I like it here."

She smiled. "I do too."

There was a knock at the door.

"Come in, Mica."

Mica and Desiree entered the room, then closed the door behind them.

Mica held up his hand. "Drake, before you begin, can I say something?"

Drake nodded. "Sure, what is it?"

"I thought you said that we wouldn't be subjected to anymore summons. We no more than got home then were called right back out here."

Drake laughed. "I did, didn't I?"

"I don't see what's so funny."

"Mica, I called you here to give you Texas. I can't think of a better person to rule than you and your mate. I would rather have a friend than foe at the helm. What do you say?"

"Texas is a large kingdom."

Drake nodded. "Yes, but a kingdom without a ruler, or subjects for that matter at the moment. Your mate had a hand in destroying the entire clan. You are charged with building your own armies just as I did. Do you think you're up to it?

"I would be honored."

"Good. We will miss having you around, but we will see you from time to time. After all, we are friends and our mates are related."

"Thank you, sire. This is the last thing I expected."

"Just be a good, strong ruler. You are my firstborn. Make me proud."

***

Sherry snuggled closer to Drake beneath the sheets. "That was a very nice thing you did tonight, love."

"Say it again."

She laughed softly. "You want me to repeat myself?"

"I never tire of hearing you say it."

She giggled. "Love, love, love, love." She propped up on an elbow. "I love you, Drake."

He flipped her over on her back and buried his cock deep between her soft folds. He wrapped her legs around his hips. "You asked me once if you could keep me."

"I did."

"I've decided that I'm never letting you go, sire."

"Good."

He covered her mouth with his and made love to her, mind, body and soul.

Karen Fuller

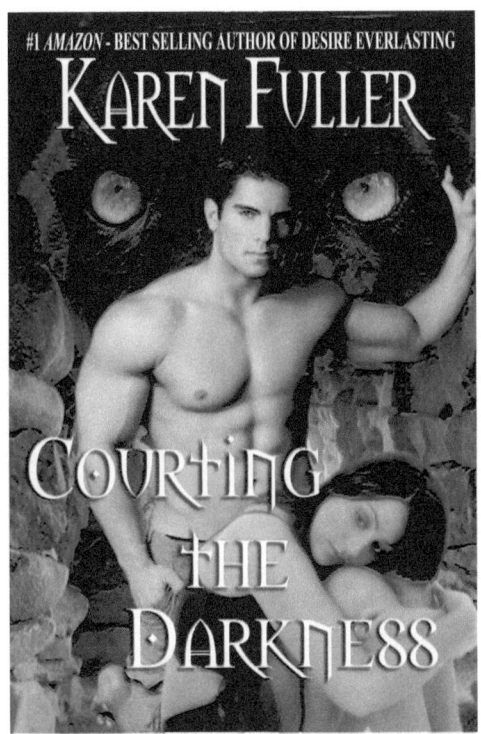

Karen Fuller

About the Author

As an Author, I love romance. Paranormal Romance happens to be a favorite of mine. I've always been an avid reader and a few years ago I discovered my passion for writing as well. I live in the Panhandle of Florida, the Sunshine State. I've been happily married to a wonderful man for the last twenty-five years. I have two grown children and 1 grandchild. When I am not writing and running my own publishing company I can be found camping with my husband or attending a NASCAR race. Please visit my websites. I am always adding something new.

http://www.karenfullerauthor.com or
http://www.worldcastlepublishing.com